To Deepak + Mel,
May you have adventures
& Blessings Always!

J. Bradford Hawk

THE ADVENTURES OF HOOD AND FUDD

THE ADVENTURES OF HOOD AND FUDD

Taming the Eastern Frontier

J. Bradford Lawler
illustrated by Kelly Cleary

Capital City Books

Capital City Books LLC

ISBN 978-0-9842881-4-4
Library of Congress Control Number 2010931113

Capital City Books LLC
Richmond, Virginia
www.capitalcitybooks.com

With much appreciation, I would like to thank my parents, Jay and Kathy Lawler. Both have gone to great lengths to shape my character, regardless of the questionable results. To my dad a special thanks for the years we spent hunting on the land where this story takes place.

To my wife, Veronica, and my daughter, Katy, thank you for your unending patience as I bombarded you with my ideas and enthusiasm.

To my friend, Brad McCord, a special thanks for reading my unedited version and mercilessly pointing out its many weaknesses.

To my sister, Kelly, the illustrations you created are fantastic and add so much to the character of the book. I'm thrilled for the opportunity to showcase your talent.

Many thanks also to my friends at Capital City Books who agreed completely with my friend Brad and slayed my work like no other. You have helped bring my work to life, and I am truly thankful.

I also thank you, the reader. I hope you enjoy reading this as much as I enjoyed writing it.

TABLE OF CONTENTS

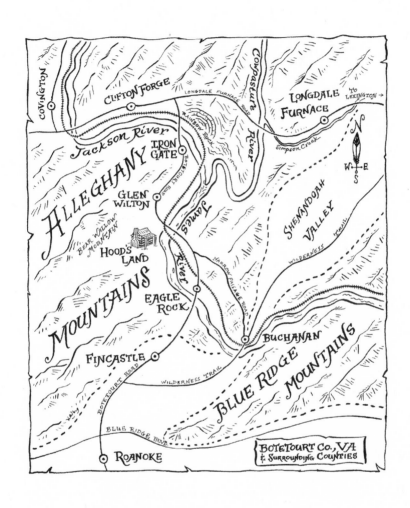

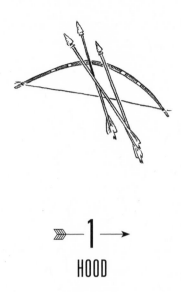

≫—1—→
HOOD

THE HALF-BREED moved only when the wind blew. The breeze rustling through the trees helped to mask his movements. You eat to live, you kill to eat. Survival is the goal of every living and breathing creature. You make a mistake, it may cost you. The woods of Appalachia are full of beauty, life and death. Nothing goes to waste. Buzzards got to eat too. The forests are ripe with danger, even if you dwell near the top of the food chain.

Silently, he crossed the property line. He was on his family's land for the first time since he'd been forced to flee with his mother and little sister four years ago. The exhilaration of setting foot once more on his father's soil gave his senses a rush of clarity. The sights and sounds of the forest seemed more vivid than before. His ears twitched as he heard the groaning wheels and felt the familiar rumble of the train on the other side of the river. It was performing its daily task of moving the coal along the base of Bear Wallow Mountain to far-off destinations. He had hopped that train often in the past, clinging to the ladder on the side of a coal car. As he watched the train, he could see the thick, grey smoke billowing from the smokestack high above the tree line. He dropped his eyes and scanned his immediate surroundings. Everything looked the same, but somehow it felt different. Nevertheless, he was home and his dinner stood just out of range.

His arrow was knocked up but he wasn't quite in position or near enough to draw his bow. He felt a slight rush of adrenaline and his mouth went dry. He had to concentrate to control his breathing. He could feel every stick and pebble through the skins of his moccasins.

He looked and felt more like a Cherokee now than ever before. His upbringing among the white settlers seemed like a distant memory, like a chapter from somebody else's life. It was the fate of the Cherokee that seemed to embrace him now. Had his life not been so violently altered at age eleven, he would be hunting this deer with a rifle instead of a bow. He would be just another boy going to school instead of an unwanted "savage."

He no longer wore the denim pants and flannel shirts that came from stores in town. His mother, Sequoia, and his younger sister, Cher, had hand-fashioned the deer skin pants and vest that adorned him now. The deer whose skins he wore had fed his family for two weeks near the end of this past winter. He felt great regard for the deer; to him, they were noble beings, just like all the creatures of the forest.

His vest slid slightly out of place, but he knew he couldn't fix it without revealing his position. All of his clothes had been made a little too big due to a recent growth spurt. The chilly October winds would be upon him soon anyway, so he was grateful that he would be able to layer some additional clothing underneath his skins. His battered bowler hat was a direct contradiction to his outfit, but it was a gift from his Pops, and it fit him now. His long, wavy, black hair streamed out from underneath.

Most people who knew him called him Hood. Others called him Indian or Half-Breed. That didn't bother him though. It didn't hurt anymore. Names were just words. Bullets had a much more painful effect. How long had it been since Pops was gunned down? Four years? He was fifteen now, soon to be sixteen. It was hard to believe that Pops had been gone for so long.

The deer walked forward a few paces and stopped. A large tree blocked its view, so Hood made a bold move. He took four quick, silent steps and drew his bow. The deer took another step and Hood instantly froze. If the deer moved just a little closer, he would have a perfect shot.

The wind shifted and Hood felt the breeze flow along the back of his neck. This was not a good development. His scent might give his position away and spoil his dinner plans. The six-point buck raised his nose into the wind. Hood could only watch as the deer's tail slowly rose up into the white flag that signaled its alert to danger. He suppressed a rueful snicker as he thought, "If deer were easy to kill, then they would be extinct."

The buck snorted audibly and dashed for safer territory. It appeared to make its way down toward the river. Hood raised himself from his shooter's stance and kicked the twig-covered earth with his moccasined toe. Hunt over; deer wins. No fresh venison tonight.

"Oh well," Hood announced in resignation. "I'll go to the river. Looks like a fine evening to fry up some fish." He still had six hooks and thirty feet of string that Rigger had sold him in exchange for a beaver skin.

Rigger was a logger, trapper and trader and could have caught all the beaver he wanted, but he seemed to like trading with "the boy" as he liked to call Hood. In the cold season, Rigger always wore a red lumberjack shirt that fit snuggly on his huge frame. In days gone by, Rigger had traded with Hood's father, Jake. Hood had often accompanied his Pops to barter with the woodsman, and Rigger had impressed both Pops and "the boy" as a man who was square and fair to deal with. Even as a young boy, Hood appreciated the respect that Rigger showed his father. Unlike many townspeople, Rigger didn't seem to mind that Pops had married a Cherokee woman or that Hood was the product of that marriage.

Why was it that some people carried no malice in their hearts and rightly judged a man based on his merits, while other people carried a venomous hatred and fear based on nothing but the circumstances of one's birth? Love and hate were dispensed due to affiliation with a group and not the character of the individual man. Hood didn't envy anyone who carried the burden of all that hate. These heavy thoughts weighed him down, so he let them pass.

With a sigh, Hood snapped his attention from the past to the present. "Catchin' worms and fish is easier than shootin' a deer," he thought. About an hour of good light remained. It was time to make some tracks. He could be at the river in half an hour with enough time to set up a camp for the night and prepare the tools he would need to fish. But first, he would have to backtrack a quarter mile to where he had tied off Oliver, his pack mule.

Hood reached the river with plenty of good light left. The sun's rays were beginning to wane. He let Oliver's lead rope dangle to the ground so the mule could do a bit of grazing. Hood removed the packs and bedroll from Oliver's back and gave him a friendly smack on the behind. Oliver, in return, tried to give Hood a playful nip in the thigh, but Hood evaded the assault. "That mule is predictable every time," Hood thought with a smile.

After he located his hooks and string, he sought and found a small river birch. Hood drew a ten-inch Bowie knife from its sheath and carved off a long branch to use as his fishing pole.

All that remained was to find some worms, and that would be a simple task. Worms were everywhere in the soft, silty banks that bordered the mouth of the James River. At least that's what white people called the river. They had named the river after one of their kings, a king of England. That same river was known as the Powhatan River to all those who belong to the Cherokee nation. The river had been named after a great chief of days past. He wasn't even a Cherokee chief, yet his name carried great respect among the Eastern tribes. It seemed funny that men of such diverse backgrounds all preferred to name this mighty river after a mighty man.

≫—2—→
FUDD

FUDD MOVED through the forest like an experienced woodsman, though not quite with the grace of an Indian. He was no tenderfoot in the art of survival. He was coming into his own and was feeling much more confident as his coordination caught up with his body. He wasn't as goofy and awkward as he had been just a year ago. His frame was taller and stronger, his fiery red hair had darkened considerably and his voice no longer squeaked when he spoke. At school he was gaining a reputation as a serious rodeo competitor, an outstanding marksman and a skilled hunter. His Hawkins .50 caliber rifle was locked and loaded. He could see the six-point buck about 200 yards away, but he wanted a better shot. His dog, Buddy, was sitting at full attention where he had been commanded to "sit."

Fudd stepped lightly off the path and onto a rock shelf. He didn't take his eyes off the deer. Slowly, he put one foot in front of the other. He was so intent on his target that he didn't hear the warning until it was too late. The yellow timber rattler sprung and struck in the shadow of a second. Fudd was bitten in the back of the calf, just above his boot. With the surge of pain came sudden enlightenment—the hunt no longer mattered.

Buddy covered the distance between him and the snake in an instant, but the damage had already been done. With bared teeth and raised hackles, he skirted around to the backside of the retreating snake and clamped down just above its rattle, shaking the viper viciously before slinging it into the rocks. He barked excitedly at the snake's motionless body before turning his attention to his wounded master.

★ ★ ★

Hood had just caught his first fish when he heard an eruption of excited barks. The sound was urgent and close. He figured he'd better investigate. With a slight hunger pang in his gut, he tossed the large bass back into the river. He looked at Oliver but decided that he could blend into his surroundings better if he traveled alone. If there was danger afoot, he didn't want to be a walking target. He gathered up his back pouch and bow and made his way toward the commotion. Curiosity led him down a path he didn't expect.

★ ★ ★

Fudd was in serious trouble and he knew it. He was four or five miles from the town of Iron Gate and the nearest doctor. The exertion of trekking there on foot would send the poison racing through his system. He leaned his rifle against a tree and angrily tossed his duster coat and trail hat beside it. He would have to get as much of the poison out as he could on his own.

Fudd sat on the ground and removed his boot. Then, he drew a ten-inch Bowie knife from the sheath on his belt. Beginning at the cuff, he sliced his pant leg all the way to the knee and exposed the wound. He hoped he would live to enjoy the day when he sewed his pant leg back together. After a quick examination, he wasted no time being squeamish about digging the knife into his flesh. He had to get the wound to bleed out as much poison as possible.

He tried to contort his body so he could suck on the wound and get out additional poison, but it was an awkward angle and he couldn't do it. He grimaced as he edged the tip of the knife in a little deeper. If he couldn't suck the poison out, then he would have to bleed it out. The irony of his predicament was that if he cut too deep, he wouldn't be able to walk back to civilization and get the help he needed. Drawing a deep breath and gritting his teeth against the sting, he deepened the cut of the other fang mark as well. The blood flowed freely, and two red trails began to stain his sock.

Fudd looked at the wound and shook his head with dissatisfaction. "I could die right here. I may be done." He looked around to see if it was a spot worthy of his death.

★ ★ ★

Hood watched on as the injured boy struggled to tend to his leg. By the way he used his knife, Hood could tell that the boy was an experienced hunter with a stubborn streak. His anger and determination were readily apparent, and Hood held back a smile. This boy was by no means ready to lie down and die. Hood shuffled a little, weighing his impulse to help against his fear that, even in an injured state, this boy might be as dangerous as a wounded bear.

Suddenly, Fudd's wandering gaze locked on Hood. Their eyes met and both boys froze, not quite sure how to react. With his presence exposed, Hood stepped out from behind the tree with his bow half drawn but the arrow pointing down. Fudd eyed his Hawkins gun leaning against the tree, just out of reach.

"This is royal! What else can go wrong?" Fudd said, not in the least bit under his breath.

Buddy advanced towards Hood slowly, the fur on the back of his neck raised and bristling. He emitted a threatening, guttural growl and positioned himself directly in front of his master. He stood stock-still, poised for an attack.

Fudd said slowly, "Don't shoot my dog."

"Call him off," Hood shot back.

Fudd complied, delivering the order in a firm tone, "Buddy, sit!"
Buddy sat, but his eyes remained fully focused on Hood.

Fudd sized up the oddly dressed intruder, trying to gauge his
intentions. "If you shoot me, he will be all over you before you can
knock up another arrow."

"I don't mean to stick ya," said Hood with a grin. "I reckon you're
having a bad enough day already. You've been snake bit. I can help if
ya want."

"Why should you help me?" asked Fudd, wondering why an Indian
would offer to help a white settler.

Hood shrugged and said, "Because you need it."

They stared at each other for a few seconds. Fudd had very little
to lose at this point. "Buddy, lie down!" he commanded. Buddy
immediately obeyed his owner's wishes. "That dang viper bit me in the
back of the leg. I can't reach it good."

Hood stepped forward and Buddy started his guttural growl again.
"Shut up, dog," Fudd cut him off.

Hood approached cautiously and laid his bow and pack on the
ground. After examining the wound, he looked up at Fudd and said,
"I'm gonna have to suck out the poison."

"Do it!" said Fudd, nodding his head. He knew what needed to be
done if he were to survive.

Hood pinched a large hunk of flesh around the wound and sucked
hard over top of each fang mark and cut. Fudd flinched from the pain,
arching his back as his palms gripped the ground, but otherwise, he
made no remark.

Hood spit the bloody poison into the dirt and wiped his mouth with
the back of his hand. The expression on his face was one of revulsion.

"Tastes pretty nasty," Hood said.

"Would that be the poison or my blood?" Both boys snickered at
Fudd's joke, even though it was no joking matter.

"Well, I've tasted blood before. That's my first time with venom." Hood reached into his pack pouch and pulled out a rag, ripped it in half and tied the first half tightly to Fudd's calf, two inches above the wound. He tied the second strip directly to the wound.

"That should help slow down the flow of the poison. Where do you want me to get ya to?" asked Hood.

"Iron Gate, I guess," said Fudd. "That's where the doc lives."

Hood hesitated for just a moment. He hated the thought of going into town. He knew he would be a target there, but it would be late by the time they arrived. Maybe he could get in and out quickly under the cover of darkness. After weighing the risks, Hood nodded a quick 'yes' to Fudd, and he gathered up their belongings.

"We should look for some good sticks to make a tow," said Hood. "You'll pass out before we get there."

Hood tossed Fudd a ball of twine from his pack pouch. "You sit right there and do the lashing while I gather the sticks we need. The less you move around the better."

Fudd nodded in agreement, as he was beginning to feel the first effects of the poison.

Hood used his Bowie knife to chop down two small poplar trees that were about two inches thick, and then he cut them to a length of ten feet. He moved with purpose, only concerned with the tow's function and not its neatness. He stripped the branches from the trunk, leaving two strong poles for the tow's support frame.

Fudd laid the support sticks beside him on the ground so that the bottom was about three feet wide and the top one foot. Hood stripped the branches and gathered other small saplings nearby until he had about fifteen sticks. He tossed them to Fudd as he completed them and Fudd sat there and did the lashing. As they neared completion of the tow, Fudd started feeling groggy and disoriented.

Hood thought of running back to his camp and fetching Oliver, as it was a long hike to Iron Gate. Even with Oliver's help dragging the boy, the going would be slow. The railroad tracks, however, crossed the river only a half-mile from where they were.

"Does the evening train still come through just after dark?" Hood inquired.

"It sure does," Fudd responded enthusiastically. He knew just what his new Indian friend had in mind. "The train could get us there real quick."

Fudd laid his trail duster jacket like a blanket in the makeshift basket that was to support him on the tow. He looked towards Hood but had trouble focusing on him—everything seemed to be pitching and spinning. He dropped to his knees and groaned, "I'm startin' to feel kind of sick."

With effort, Fudd rolled onto the sled and Hood packed their belongings around him. He hoisted up the head of the sled and put the ends of the support beams on his shoulders. Leaning forward, he strained against the weight as the other end of the support beams dragged on the ground. They had to get moving; time was of the essence.

As Fudd became more delirious, he began to talk to himself and laugh at his situation. He was literally laughing in the face of death. Hood respected the grit of his character and wondered if he himself would be able to face death with such nobility.

The boy interrupted his thoughts to inquire, "We ain't had much time for formalities, but I 'spect I'd like to know your name."

"Hood."

Fudd craned his neck a little and looked at the back of Hood's head. "I've heard of you. You used to go to my school before we came to town. My family settled in Glen Wilton three years ago. Word is that your dad got shot and the rest of your family was run off because ya'll were a mixed family, half white and half Indian."

"I'm not Indian," said Hood defiantly. "I'm Cherokee," he hesitated, "and Irish. And this half-breed is trying to save your life."

Fudd laughed a quick laugh and smiled, "I don't mean no offense. If I don't make it, let me say right here and now, that opinion don't hold true to me. And I say thanks for trying to save my life. My name's Fudd."

Hood smiled in spite of himself. He was beginning to like this kid. He said nothing though, and continued to reveal little of himself, but he called on a little extra strength and pulled harder. A misty rain began to mix with the sweat that had formed on his face, and the light of the day waned into darkness.

Buddy sensed that Hood was here to help. He no longer felt the need to defend and protect his master. He seemed to know where they were going and ran point on the path in front of Hood. He never got in the way or slowed Hood down. Hood thought to himself, "That is one good dog."

The dog plodded along at the head of the small caravan. From a distance, Hood could almost mistake him for a small black bear—big chest, curly tail, threatening mouth, bushy black fur and kinda cute. Hood thought he might be part Chow and part black Lab, with the temperament of either, depending on the situation. He thought it was odd that no one seemed to care when a dog was a mixed breed.

Fudd was starting to moan occasionally. He was also talking a bit less. "I'm fifteen years old," Fudd said. "How old are you?"

"Sixteen," Hood lied. Why did he lie? It wasn't his habit to lie. It wasn't a matter of survival either. He had been taught better by his Pops and by Chief Namar. He was proud of who and what he was. He corrected himself. "I'm fifteen actually. I'll be sixteen in a week or two. What is today's date anyway?"

"Tuesday," Fudd responded.

That didn't help much.

"When we get to town, do you know where the doc lives?"

"Yep," said Hood.

They were halfway to the bridge that would bring the train to their side of the river when Fudd said, "I'm gonna pass out soon. Thanks, Hood. You would make a good friend."

Those were the last words Fudd spoke that night, and they echoed in Hood's head. Man, he hoped Fudd would make it.

DRIVER 8

HOOD HAD been dragging Fudd for an hour when he heard the rumble of the oncoming train. He quickened his pace. If he could get the train to stop, then Fudd would get to the doctor much quicker. It was the best chance that Fudd would have.

The light from the engine splashed over the three of them as Hood positioned them next to the tracks. Hood could see the big number eight on the front of the engine as it rapidly approached. Everyone had always called the engineer of the number eight train "Driver 8" and Hood realized that he didn't even know his real name. Hood stood with one foot on the rail waving and yelling frantically. If Driver 8 was stoking the fire, he might never know they were there. Even if he did notice them, he might think it was a ruse to stop the train for a robbery.

As the train bore down on them, there was no evidence that it was planning to slow down, and Hood had to jump out of the way at the last possible second. His heart sank as the engine rolled past. What were they going to do now?

Then the air brakes hissed and the train whistle sounded two quick blasts. Steam was spewing in all directions. The train was slowing down!

Hood felt an incredible sense of relief. The odds of Fudd surviving the night had just improved.

Driver 8 appeared from the front of the train and the conductor came around from the rear.

"Why did you stop the train?" asked the conductor in a gruff tone. As soon as the steam cleared, Hood could see who the conductor was—Colonel Deacon Sanders, dressed in his customary white outfit. He had fought in the Civil War and his unit had surrendered after a minor skirmish. Hood hadn't laid eyes on him in years, but the Colonel still looked like an upper-crust dandy with his immaculately groomed white goatee to match his white ensemble. Hood suspected that the Colonel wore that crisp white suit out of a desire to distinguish himself from the dusty-dungareed farmers and workers who he looked down on. Others, however, joked that he wore white to save the time of pulling out a white flag of surrender. The Colonel was known to be a chicken.

Driver 8 responded, "It looks like we have an injured young man."

Hood began to explain, "This is Fudd, and he's been snake-bit."

The Colonel looked Hood over and glanced at the nearly unconscious Fudd. "We don't allow Indians on the train."

"That's Jake Hood's boy," Driver 8 intervened.

"So?" the Colonel retorted. "What're you doin' back in these parts anyway, Half-Breed?"

"I live here," said Hood. "In fact, my fathers and forefathers have been living in these mountains since before your father was born."

"Fathers and forefathers," the Colonel mocked. "This half-breed even talks like an injun. Forefathers is called ancestrials, you idjit."

Hood didn't bother to correct the Colonel. He saw no point.

Driver 8 laughed and responded, "The kid gets a free ride. Now get back to your post, we need to get on down the track. Mr. Fudd here looks like he needs a doctor. And Colonel, put all three in the empty cattle car next to the caboose."

"All three?" questioned the Colonel.

"Yeah. We're giving the dog a free ride too."

The Colonel gave an abrupt, "Humph," and spun on his heels.

As the Colonel unlocked the cattle car door, Driver 8 helped Hood carry Fudd toward the rear of the train.

"Riding in the car instead of on the side ladder will be a switch for you, won't it boy?" said Driver 8.

With a sheepish grin, Hood looked up into the friendly face and changed the subject: "Thank you for your help, sir. Your kindness will probably save his life."

They strained to hoist Fudd up to the Colonel, but eventually managed. After Fudd came Buddy, who Hood picked up and heaved through the opening. He handed up the tow sled and then mounted the ladder, launching himself through the open door.

The Colonel gave Hood one last disapproving look before he descended the ladder to the ground. He walked back to the caboose and gave a double ring on his bell. The engineer rang his own bell twice in response, and the train started to creep forward. They only had about three miles to Iron Gate and six miles to Clifton Forge. Iron Gate wasn't a scheduled stop, but it would be a stop tonight.

≫—4—→
THE STRANGER

BIG RUSTY Grimm eyed the shotgun again. Rusty was the bartender and proprietor of the Dew Drop Inn. The Dew Drop was the only drinking and gambling establishment in the town of Iron Gate, and it provided a comfortable place for people to socialize, plus a whole row of rooms to rent on the second floor. Although the building was old, it was well cared for. It and the Trading Post next door were the oldest businesses in town. Generally, as the evenings wore on, the Inn attracted patrons of a rougher kind.

Rusty casually cleaned a glass with a rag so he wouldn't look so nervous. He particularly hated when Emmett Stone and his gang of Cowboys came to town. Artimus Aikman and Lazarus Lett were never far away from Emmett; they were his main sidekicks. This particular night, Emmett was drunk and losing at cards, and that was usually a bad combination.

Rusty casually opened a box of 12-gauge shotgun shells and set them next to the shotgun. He knew it was loaded; he had checked when Emmett and the Cowboys came through the swinging doors.

Sitting to Emmett's right was a broad-shouldered man with round spectacles and a thick mustache. Rusty hadn't seen him in these parts before. If he had, he might have warned the stranger to stay away from Emmett, whose face was growing redder by the minute.

The stranger didn't seem to notice though. He stared cooly down at his hand as he continued to take Emmett's money. This behavior provoked Emmett all the more.

"Two pairs. Aces and eights," announced the stranger as he laid his cards down for the others to see.

"Dead Man's Hand," said Lazarus with a cackle as he thought of Wild Bill Hickok's famous last words before he was murdered during a card game.

Artimus closed the fan of cards in his hands abruptly and then threw them face down toward Emmett. It was Emmett's turn to deal next. Artimus leaned back in his chair and lit a small cigar.

"That would be three hands in a row," observed Artimus with a sneer.

As Emmett continued to stew in his anger, Artimus leaned forward and addressed the stranger more directly, "You Northern gents must know some tricks about cards that elude us here in the South." The stranger understood that the comment was intended as an attack on his character.

Emmett kept staring at his pair of kings and queens but they refused to improve under his searing gaze. With disgust, he tossed them on top of Artimus's cards.

Lazarus gently laid his card face down on the discard pile and spit at the spittoon. He missed, almost hitting the stranger's foot. They made eye contact and the stranger raked in his money from the middle of the table.

Finally, the expected outburst came. Emmett angrily swept the cards off of the table, scattering them across the saloon floor.

"I ain't never seen such luck in all my days!" Emmett scanned the faces of his cronies, looking for a reason to take it to a new level.

"Are you suggesting that I'm a cheat?" the stranger asked with a level of calm that seemed, to Big Rusty, a little unsettling.

Emmett smiled and showed off his gold front teeth. His two friends grinned wickedly and began to stand, but the stranger was much faster than the Cowboys.

He had two pistols drawn so fast that the smiles were still frozen on their faces. Emmett could feel the chill of cold steel as the barrel pressed into his upper lip, just under his nose. He could see the heads of the bullets as they waited in the cylinder of the stranger's cavalry-issued Colt .44 revolver. The stranger held the other two gamblers at bay with the gun in his right hand.

Everyone in the bar stopped dead in their tracks. Even the piano player quit playing. The stranger stood slowly and deliberately.

Politely, he stated, "I think I'll be taking my leave now. Does anyone object?" All three men shook their heads no.

"Mr. Bartender," said the stranger.

"Yes, sir?" Rusty replied.

"I don't really care to make a mess here in your establishment. Would you be so kind as to gather my money and pay for all the drinks for me and my friends here?"

Big Rusty eyed the shotgun again. He had never even had a chance to make a grab for it. To try now would be suicide.

"Yes, sir," said Rusty again as he left the protective sanctuary that the bar provided. His hands shook as he collected the money. Rusty nervously looked up at the stranger and questioned meekly, "Pay for all the drinks?"

The stranger gave a single nod of his head. "Take a five dollar bill for yourself. Also, Mr. Bartender, would you be kind enough to relieve these gentlemen of their weapons and dump the shells on the floor?"

The stranger pushed the pistol further into the flesh of Emmett's face and forced him to back up a few steps into the middle of the room.

Rusty placed the stranger's money in a tidy stack on the table. He walked by each of the Cowboys and slowly drew the pistols out of each holster by the butt. He unloaded each and tossed the shells and guns on the floor. Emmett was fuming mad and stared Rusty down. Rusty backed away with trepidation, hoping that Emmett wouldn't blame him for the offense.

"If I was to see anyone run out that front door, I might be tempted to shoot first and ask questions later," the stranger warned as he holstered his left gun and picked up his money. He backed toward the swinging saloon doors. "Good evening to all," he said with a curt little nod and a tip of his hat. And he was gone.

⇛─5─→
THE GOOD DOCTOR OF IRON GATE

THE WEATHER had changed for the worse. It was a dark and stormy night. The street lanterns served as beacons only; their dim glow did little to illuminate the streets. The doctor's house was on the edge of town, at the opposite end of the street from the saloon. A light shone from his downstairs window. Since the street was deserted, Hood decided he would take Fudd straight to the doctor's front door, instead of skirting around the edge of town to avoid detection.

Before proceeding, Hood hid his personal belongings between a fence and a small bush and then hung Fudd's pack and rifle on a post. Fudd was passed out completely, so Hood pulled him off the sled and slung him over his shoulder like a large sack of potatoes. Fudd moaned slightly and Hood supposed that that was a good sign. After grabbing Fudd's possessions, Hood loosened the tie-down to his knife in case he was suddenly confronted with trouble. Vulnerable, he felt very vulnerable. Burdened by Fudd's weight, he scooted down the street as fast as he could. Buddy shot out ahead of him.

★ ★ ★

Lazarus Lett walked out the side door of the saloon and into the alley. He turned and watered the side wall of the Trading Post. He couldn't believe that stranger got the jump on him and Emmett and Artimus! He was still mad and looking for a fight. As he turned to go back inside, he caught a glimpse of a man carrying another man on his shoulders.

"Great," he muttered to himself, "Always something goin' on in this boring little town." He walked to the front of the alley and watched as the straining figure carried his load to the doctor's front steps. He never considered offering to help.

★ ★ ★

The good doctor of Iron Gate had lived in the same house for the past thirty years. He was fifty-five now, and feeling his age. Arthritis was in his knees, not his fingers, thank the good Lord! His wife, Martha, was upstairs asleep in their apartment above his office. To think of all the babies he had delivered, and they were never able to have one of their own. But who could understand the troubles of life? A child he had delivered fourteen years ago had died this very day and there had been nothing he could do, as she had already passed from her wounds. His mood was somber. He pulled off his glasses and rubbed his eyes. The dim lighting had put a strain on them, causing a headache. His lamp was low on oil, but he was too tired to refill it.

A tapping at his window startled him and he looked up to see a wet face staring through it. "Is that Jedediah Hood?" he wondered as he put his glasses on and moved quickly to the door.

"He's snake-bit, Doc Larick! He says his name is Fudd."

"That's Fudd all right," said the doctor. "I'm fixin' that boy up all the time. Help me get him on the couch, will ya, son?"

Hood grabbed Fudd underneath his shoulders while the doctor took his feet, and they hoisted him gently onto the couch.

"Do you know the type of snake that bit him?" the doctor asked as he examined the wound.

"Rattler."

"The yellow timber rattlesnake is the most common around these parts," the doctor surmised, bringing his hand to his chin. "Do you think that was it?"

"I believe it was," Hood recollected, wishing he had taken a closer look.

The doctor moved quickly and efficiently but wanted to talk to Hood as he worked. Hood was anxious to get out of town.

"It's been a while since I've see you, Jedediah. How are you?" asked Doc Larick.

"Okay, I guess," said Hood, shifting uncomfortably and glancing toward the window.

"I'm sorry I couldn't save your daddy that day," Doc said as he mixed a murky solution in a glass jar.

"It warn't your fault, Doc. You didn't shoot him."

"Are your mother and sister well?"

"Their health is good," Hood responded. "Our tribe has been living in union with the Monacan tribe at God's Bridge near Lexington. The Sheriff of Big Lick is trying to force what remains of both tribes down to a reservation in the Carolinas. Oh, I guess Big Lick is called Roanoke now." Hood shrugged, wondering why the white man had used an Iroquois name. "My grandfather has kept the tribe there, but he feels that time is short until we will be forced to move or fight. To fight would mean the death of the tribe."

"Ah, Chief Namar is as wise as ever. So many tribes have been forced to move or disband," Doc said as he tore a clean rag into thin bandaging strips. "It is a tribute to your grandfather that the tribe has remained intact for this long."

"Grandfather has taught me many things that he fears will be lost. For his entire life, he's watched the Cherokee grow smaller and the white man grow larger. He feels the Cherokee life will soon be gone forever. He would have me grow up with the white man and learn their wisdom."

The doctor could sense the turmoil in Hood's words. "And how do you feel?"

"No offense, but I'm not so sure I want to be white anymore. The death of my father and life with the tribe has made me more grateful for simple pleasures. Now, I feel happier in buckskin. I am at peace with the forest. I value the gift of life and not the attainment of things. I live with the people and creatures that accept me. The Lord is my shepherd, not my excuse to take what isn't mine."

The doctor nodded in acknowledgement and continued his work. Fudd flinched even though he didn't wake as the doctor swabbed the solution onto his wound. "It would appear that you have gained some of the Chief's wisdom even if you don't wish to return to the settler's ways as he would like."

"To be a settler, I must be accepted as a settler. Some folks will accept me for who I am and others will always see me as a half-breed." Hood felt a familiar rage grip him, but he did his best to tuck it back into the recesses of his heart. Anger and rage belonged on the battlefield and not in the conversation of peaceful men. He took a few deep breaths and calmed himself.

After the doctor bandaged the wound, he walked to a stack of shelves lined with small bottles of different colors and shapes and grabbed a blue one. He turned to Hood, "This would be easier if he were awake." The doctor opened the bottle and poured a measured amount into a metal cup. Then he opened Fudd's mouth and poured it in. Fudd tossed slightly, but the doctor kept pressure on his chin until he reflexively swallowed.

After a spell, Hood walked out onto Doc Larick's front porch. Buddy looked at him expectantly. His tail wagged, and Hood enjoyed the feeling of acceptance. He bent forward and rubbed Buddy's head behind his right ear. The dog moved closer and pressed his head against Hood's thigh. Hood sat down on the top porch step and scratched under Buddy's snout. They both stared into the dark and dismal night and enjoyed a moment of peaceful thought.

The doctor walked out onto the porch and took a seat next to Hood. "Ruben will be all right. He's a big, strong kid."

"Ruben?" questioned Hood. "He said his name was Fudd."

"It is," said the Doc. "Ruben Fudd."

From far off, a coyote howled, and the three turned to gaze unseeingly in the direction of the sound.

"Here's his gun, his pack and his dog," Hood said. "I want to get out of town before Emmett Stone finds out I'm here."

The doctor nodded and smiled, "That's probably in your best interest. He's a mean old goat, that Emmett." His demeanor turned serious. "I know you've had a rough go of it since your daddy died. I hope you consider me a friend. If there's any way I can help, you just let me know."

"Pops didn't die," Hood stated. "He was murdered."

The doctor just nodded his head in acknowledgement. He could sense the pain that Hood did not want to share.

"I best be getting out of town," said Hood.

They stood facing each other. The doctor stuck out his hand and Hood shook it.

"Take care of yourself, Jedediah."

"That's the plan," said Hood, and he was swallowed by the night.

➤➤ 6 →
DOWNTOWN AT MIDNIGHT

HOOD TOOK the back alleys to where his pack and bow were stashed by the fence. He was thirty paces away when Emmett and Artimus stepped out of the dark, ten yards in front of him, pistols drawn. He turned his head and, sure enough, there was Lazarus, ten yards behind him. How could he be so stupid as to let these idiots get the drop on him?

"We've missed you, Half-Breed," said Emmett, smiling.

Hood could see Emmett's gold teeth flash in the dim light as he spun the cylinder of his Smith and Wesson, cocking his ear towards the clicking sound.

His smile grew wider and more ominous.

Hood slowly drew his knife. It was the only weapon he had on him.

"Ain't that just like a stupid, stinkin' redskin." The venom in Emmett Stone's voice was enough to make Hood's skin crawl. "Bringin' a knife to a gun fight." All three Cowboys cackled with delight.

"Look how he's dressed," said Lazarus. "He done turned completely Indian, 'cept for that hat. I think I might like that hat after we're done with 'em."

"I'm a Cherokee, not an Indian," replied Hood. His eyes scanned the sneering faces of each Cowboy. "I'll fight you all, one at a time."

"I don't believe you make the rules," said Artimus in his dandy-like manner. He was a true Doc Holliday wanna-be. He dressed in fancy, tight-fitting, black clothing. His shirt was white with a thin, black string tie. His hat was very stylish, not typical of the crowds that he ran with. No doubt, he was lean and mean and he looked the part.

"In fact, there are no rules. It would appear that you are at a disadvantage." He put his left hand to his face and stroked his cheek twice, while his right index finger caressed the trigger of his pistol. "My, oh *my*," he said.

Artimus got an unnatural thrill from killing. He no longer knew the exact number of people he had killed—people, not just men. Women and children were not off limits by any means. He killed to suit his purpose, and he avoided justice by leaving no witnesses other than the members of his various gangs.

Emmett Stone spun the cylinder of his Smith and Wesson and cocked the trigger.

Suddenly, a steely voice cut through the darkness.

"The boy's not alone," it said. A bolt of fear shot through each of the three Cowboys.

The stranger stepped into the dim light with both pistols in hand. "My guns seem to be drawn whenever you three are near. Drop your guns now, gentlemen," he commanded.

Three guns immediately hit the ground.

"Boy," said the stranger to Hood, "would you like an escort out of town?"

"No," said Hood, his heart pounding with relief. "I just want to grab my belongings. Then I'll disappear."

The stranger nodded and said, "Well, then. Get on with it!"

Hood dashed over to the fence. He slung the pack and quiver over his shoulder and walked slowly back to the standoff with one arrow knocked up in his bow. He looked up at the stranger and said, "Thanks, mister. He'd a killed me just like he killed my Pops."

Stone protested loudly, "They found me not guilty, you stinkin' half-breed. You got no cause to spread rumors like that."

"I got plenty of cause, you back-shooter!" exclaimed Hood. His face felt flush with anger.

Emmett growled with fury and took a step toward Hood.

A soft, metallic click came from the direction of the stranger, and he calmly stated, "One more step and it will be your last."

Emmett stopped in his tracks.

While the stranger was fully engaged with Emmett, Artimus edged his hand toward his waist and the spare gun tucked into his belt. His hand began to twitch with excitement as it neared the butt of his gun. The stranger had no idea he was about to die. Artimus grinned wickedly and made his move.

One single shot rang out in the night.

Beth, the Cookes' maid, screamed and dropped the bundle of clothes she was carrying. She had been oblivious to the goings on just outside her employer's door.

Blood shot out from between Artimus's fingers and stained the collar and breast of his clean white shirt. He dropped to his knees briefly, still clutching his throat, and began to spasm.

Then it was over. Artimus Aikman was dead.

Emmett stared in disbelief at his dead compadre, then he looked up at the stranger. The corners of his lips turned into a cunning grin. "You gonna hang for that one, mister."

The stranger was unperturbed by Emmett Stone's threat and casually asked, "Would you prefer that I leave no witnesses?"

The smile vanished from Emmett's face.

"Grab those guns, boy," said the stranger.

Hood did as he was told. The stranger turned back to the two remaining Cowboys.

"Start walking toward the Trading Post," he said. They looked at each other but didn't move.

"Now!" the stranger commanded, and they began to walk.

"Follow me," said the stranger to Hood, motioning in the direction opposite the departing Cowboys. Hood nodded, and together they disappeared into the night.

→7→
COFFEE

HOOD AND his new friend took their first sip of hot morning coffee. It was strong and black, how they both liked it. Hood spit a coffee ground into the fire. They had shared a camp together for the night. From their well-hidden vantage point they could see the ruins of the old Hood cabin where it sat peacefully next to the James River. It was just after dawn. The morning was cold and crisp, and mist pooled in the valley along the river. Geese could be heard honking in the distance.

"I think the best part of waking up is that first cup of coffee," the stranger tipped his cup toward Hood in the fashion of a toast.

"As long as it tastes this good," Hood said, returning the toast. "Been a while since I've had such a fine cup of coffee."

He suddenly remembered many such simple pleasures that had been removed from his life. Because the tribe was constantly being pushed from one place to another, he had been forced to give up a great deal of luxuries. Possessions were limited to what could be carried on his back or a horse.

"So this is your family land," the stranger observed as he surveyed his surroundings. "It's very beautiful this time of year. The leaves are beginning to turn."

"It's beautiful all year round," replied Hood.

Both of their heads rose as they watched a hawk weave its way through the tree branches and land on a limb not far from them. They looked back at each other and grinned, knowing that their point had just been proven.

The night before, Hood and his new friend had traded life stories. The stranger had introduced himself only by the initials T.R. As Hood observed him now over the rim of his cup of coffee, it struck him that he rarely felt such a sense of trust in anyone so quickly.

T.R. looked to be in his late twenties or early thirties. His demeanor was tough but tempered with kindness. He carried himself in a stately manner, his posture very erect. The spectacles he wore and his well-groomed mustache projected a wise authority. He was obviously well-educated and a man of means. The cowboy hat he wore sat tall and proud on his head. His clothing was of the finest quality, but made for the intended purpose of life on the trail. A chain led from his belt across his belly to a pocket that no doubt contained a pocket watch. He wore his pride with dignity, not vanity.

Hood felt that the man was full of good ideals. His character struck him as larger than life.

He and his horse, Pepper, had hopped a train from New York to hunt down the man-eating mountain lion in Clifton Forge. Word of the great cat had reached the *New York Times* newspaper, and T.R. could not resist a good adventure.

"How much land does your family own here?" T.R. asked, bringing Hood back from his thoughts.

"'Bout three hundred acres. Probably close to a mile of river front," responded Hood. "I'm here to reclaim it."

"It seems we have some folks around here that don't enjoy our company," T.R. noted.

Hood nodded his head. "Everything changes when Emmett and the Cowboys come to town. They walk down the street in a pack, and people get out of their way. They're a bunch of bullies. They make a lot of noise. They break things. They want someone to stand up against them so they have an excuse to hurt or kill them. That's what my Pops did, and they shot him in the back. If I'm to live in these parts again, then there's gonna have to be a showdown."

"Am I mistaken?" T.R. raised his eyebrows in mock confusion. "I thought there just was a showdown."

"Yeah," laughed Hood. "That's likely to put Emmett in a foul mood." He grinned from ear to ear, then his face turned dead serious. "He'll be looking for us when Sheriff Green ain't around."

"How are your skills with a pistol, Mr. Hood?"

"Mr. Hood!" repeated Hood with a prideful smile. "I don't think I've been called that before." He puffed up his chest and raised his chin in an attempt to look dignified.

T.R. laughed at the display. "Well, you're a land owner now, and I've enjoyed the hospitality of your camp, so I feel that the title is appropriate. But, back to my question, how are your skills with a pistol?"

"Not great," Hood responded more seriously. "I haven't had much practice, but I'm very good with a rifle or a bow."

"Do you own a pistol?"

"No, just the four pistols we took from those Cowboys."

"Those guns should be turned over to the Sheriff. We both need to be on the correct side of the law on this rather serious issue. A man is dead, and the law will be compelled to act. You should go to the Sheriff and present your side of the story. If you don't stay clean with the law, then you give good men a reason to come looking for you. I plan to visit the Sheriff myself. Should I tell him to expect a visit from you?"

"I'll go see him," Hood decided. "I'm not sure when, but I'll go see him soon."

T.R. seemed satisfied with Hood's answer. Then he walked over to where Pepper was lashed to a tree. Reaching into his saddlebag, he pulled out an object wrapped in a rag. He unwrapped a pistol and held it out for Hood to see.

"This is a United States Army issue .44 caliber 1860 model single action revolver with a walnut stock. I have carried this pistol for the last five years. It is a fine weapon and has saved my bacon on a couple of occasions. I have recently acquired a new pistol and only brought this along for back up and comfort. I would like for this pistol to belong to you." T.R. handed the pistol to Hood along with four boxes of shells.

T.R. looked directly into Hood's eyes. The expression on his face was one of sadness. "For most of my life I've watched the white man take from the Indian nations. Progress can be painful and unsympathetic indeed. I'd like to give something back. Use half these shells for practice and save the other half. Learn to shoot by instinct. You have to be fast and accurate. There is no second place in a gun fight."

Hood let his eyes run over the pistol's gleaming surface. It showed some signs of wear but otherwise appeared to be well cared for. It felt awkward in his hand as he planted his feet and took aim at the base of a tree. He pulled out of his shooter's stance and opened up the cylinder to see if the gun was loaded. It was not.

He smiled at T.R. and thanked him.

"So what kind of pistol do you carry now?" Hood asked, with a new curiosity in handguns.

T.R. drew the pistol from his side and handed it butt first to Hood. "It's loaded of course."

Hood nodded and noticed for the first time that the pistol was special. The grip was made of ivory and had a ten-point buck carved into the handle. He rolled the pistol over in his hand to see the other side: a buffalo. The barrel was silver plated.

"That is a Smith and Wesson .38 caliber double action revolver, model 1880. See the Smith and Wesson stamp there on the barrel?"

"Yes," Hood nodded as he studied the emblem.

"Always look for that emblem when dealing with Smith and Wesson. There are a lot of forgeries out there that do not possess the same quality as this weapon."

"It's a fine lookin' pistol, sir, and now it has saved both our bacons,"

Hood declared jovially as he handed the weapon back to its owner.

"This revolver was a gift to me for services rendered to the United States Cavalry," he said, his voice now soft and solemn. "The man who gave it to me was President Grover Cleveland."

≫—8—→
THE FUNERAL ANNOUNCEMENT

ROANOKE TIMES, *Wednesday October 9, 1888*

"Mountain Lion Strikes Again!" read the headline. Newspapers loved to print about blood and death. If it bleeds, it leads.

"The small communities of Iron Gate and Glen Wilton wail in pain once again, as they suffer yet another vicious attack by a mountain lion. This is the fourth human death in the last five months. Livestock kills in the same locale have also been reported and attributed to the same said beast.

"The most recent attack was witnessed by the victim's sister. Madeline and Patricia Gordon had been fetching water from the creek when the beast pounced from a perch above. They were within view of their home, but this did not thwart a predator that lurks in the shadows. This mountain lion is becoming bolder and more daring. Madeline frantically beat at the cat with a walking stick and turned it back into the woods, but not before Patricia had suffered more wounds than she could survive.

"Fletch Gordon, the victim's father, has upped the bounty by $100. The total reward for the dead mountain lion is now up to $600. Patricia Gordon's funeral is to take place at the Iron Gate Baptist Church on Saturday, 2:00 p.m."

⟫—9—→
OUT OF THE ASHES

HOOD GAVE T.R. a description of the mountains that surrounded them and some ideas as to where he might find the mountain lion. After T.R departed for the high country, Hood decided that it was time to finally visit his former homestead. Oliver, Hood's mule, was quickly packed with all of their belongings and off they went.

As Hood approached, he had to fight back a tear. Sorrow swept through him as the scene before him brought back memories of that evil day. Not that long ago, his family home had stood proudly near the river, just above the flood plain. The logs had been honed from massive pine trees that once stood in the now overgrown pasture. All that remained of the cabin was a burned-out husk, one corner still standing about five feet high. The corrugated tin that served as the roof had been reduced to small melted and misshapen pieces.

Hood entered the ruins where he once would have gone through the front door. Lightly, he trod through the debris toward the fireplace, careful not to cut his moccasins on the jagged bits of metal and glass. His heart ached as he thought back to that night. The chimney still stood, but was partially crumbling. It would have to be disassembled and rebuilt to regain its former strength. He found an axe head with the handle burned away. It used to lean against the stone facing, waiting to perform its duty. He could fashion a new handle out of oak and it would swing once again. He opened his back pouch and tucked the axe head near the bottom, then walked to the boundary of the former house and stepped over the foundation wall. The foundation stones, he observed, were in fine condition.

Gazing into the field, he noted that Oliver was already content to graze. The fencing around the pasture was in need of limited repair and would serve Oliver and any other livestock well. The pasture itself was overgrown with weeds and small saplings. Hood walked over to the barn and was happy to see that it had faired reasonably well. It had been set on fire, but only one corner had sustained much damage. The roof was mostly intact and would keep the rain off of his head and, for that matter, Oliver's head too. Hood could still smell a smoky funk that remained in the surviving logs. It could be made habitable, though, until the cabin could be rebuilt.

The idea of restoration made Hood stop what he was doing. It was the first time he'd thought in terms of rebuilding. Until now, he had thought only of re-staking his claim on the land he'd been forced from, taking back what was rightfully his. Now, though, as he surveyed the damage and inventoried the remains, he found himself wanting more. It would be an honor to his father if he could one day return his mother and sister to their home. They, like he, belonged to this land. It owned them more than they owned it. He decided then and there that he would make it so.

⫸—10—→
SCHOOL

TEN MORE minutes until class was out for the weekend. Katy could hardly wait. Patricia's death had hung over the classroom like a storm cloud for the last three days. Ruben was back in school for the first time since his snake-bite incident. She was glad he was okay, but she couldn't shake a feeling of anticipation. Jedediah had also returned and she felt giddy with excitement. These last four years had been lonely for her. Often, she had thought of Jedediah, and had prayed for his family's safety.

As a childhood playmate and close neighbor of the Hood family, she had seen a side of Indian life that most other people chose not to see. The Hoods had lived in a nice cabin on a fine ranch similar to the lifestyle of other settlers, but Sequoia, Hood's mother, still dressed in native attire. Members of her tribe visited and pitched in with the ranch work or harvest when help was needed.

Katy had, on occasion, visited the tribe and felt that the way they lived was noble. They were an honest race of people and she couldn't understand why some people feared them and called them savages. All the Indians she knew were kind and hospitable, even though they were often treated with scorn. Hospitality to strangers was an earmark of the

Cherokee culture, but most of the settlers never would understand that.

Katy brushed her long blond hair back behind her ears and looked out the window.

When Jedediah was in school or in town, she had seen him treated poorly on many occasions, usually when no adults were around. Zeb Henry was the worst. He liked to bark at Jedediah and call him Mutt. Shank Henry had taught his son to be just as mean and prejudiced as he was. After Hood had disappeared, Zeb constantly tried to gain Katy's affections. His manner had been rude and obnoxious, as if he expected this to impress her. When it didn't have his intended effect, he became even more rude and bullying.

He wasn't exactly stupid; he did have a certain degree of cunning, but he reminded Katy more of a weasel than a fox. He was quick-witted in a depraved and insulting manner. He actually thought he had a chance with Katy once Hood was out of the picture. Eventually, though, Zeb had dropped out of school and the rabble that always followed his lead went with him. "Good riddance," thought Katy. They really had no ambition to study or learn. They weren't much at being farm hands either. All they wanted to do was play rodeo games and stir up trouble. Why her father let him work on their ranch during the harvest she would never understand.

None of that mattered now. Jedediah was back. Katy wondered if he would be at the funeral tomorrow. He had known Patricia from when they all went to school together.

"Katy," a voice rang out, "Katy! … Miss Kathryn Highland!" Her teacher, Miss Kieran Summers, snapped her out of her daydream. Her little sister, Ellie, snickered along with most of the class. The girls were identical twins, but Katy had been born first.

Miss Summers was kind, patient and firm. She maintained excellent control of her classroom. Her students loved her. She had rapped more than a few students on the knuckles with her ruler, but mostly just the boys. When she felt the classroom was a little too rowdy, she would pick up the ruler and continue her lesson as she walked about the room.

Usually just the sight of the ruler did the trick.

She had been raised in this community and returned after her education to help this little township grow. The loves of her life were her students, her aging father, William, and her cat, Calico Kitty. Her mother had been gone for years.

She was petite and quite pleasant to look at, but she rarely flirted or even showed up at town dances. Her Baptist roots had kept her modest, although her education had allowed her progressive side to develop. She loved to learn and teach, and she was able to pass this trait on to many of her students. Even in the farming communities away from the big cities, people were beginning to see the value of an education. Other than her own mother, Katy admired Ms. Summers more than any other lady she knew. She hoped she'd grow up to be just like her.

After class was dismissed, Katy strolled out to the front of the schoolhouse. The afternoon sun was warm and bright and Calico Kitty was basking in the sun on the front porch. Next to her lay the remains of a half-eaten mouse, the head and the upper torso missing. Calico Kitty was a good mouser. Two half-grown kittens from her most recent litter played at the bottom of the steps. They no longer needed their mother for milk. The rest of the litter either had run off and become feral or had been taken by predators. Survival of the fittest, as Darwin had put it.

Last year Katy's father had travelled to Richmond. He had returned with a book authored by Charles Darwin, *The Origin of Species*. There is no doubt that Darwin was a genius, but as she looked at these kittens happily playing, unconcerned about potential danger, she felt that Darwin left out the hand of God in his equations. Survival of the fastest, meanest, smartest, luckiest and most blessed by the Lord was how she viewed life.

Katy and Ellie drew alongside Fudd as the students dispersed and went their various ways. Ellie grabbed Fudd by the elbow and said, "You certainly gave everyone a good start. We almost lost two students in the same day!"

Ellie had always had an eye for the tall and strapping redhead. Ruben Fudd had been working as a part time ranch hand for her father for over a year. Fudd looked shyly at the ground and kicked a little dirt. He held his cowboy hat in his hand.

"I got lucky that Hood feller heard Buddy barkin'. If he hadn't happened along then I'd a been buzzard bait fer sure."

"How did he look?" asked Katy, trying to sound only mildly interested.

"He looked pretty lean, but he must be strong as an ox 'cause he dragged and carried me quite a ways gettin' me to the doc."

"Everybody thinks that Emmett Stone shot his dad," added Ellie, "but he got off from it at the courthouse. Then someone burned down the cabin that his family built down past Glen Wilton."

"I was huntin' near there when I got snake bit. I seen that old burned down cabin plenty of times," said Fudd.

"He, his sister and mom just disappeared," Ellie continued. "We thought they might be dead. Then Katy got a letter from him about two years ago. He said they were livin' with the tribe outside of Big Lick. His mom is a Cherokee princess, did ya know? Chief Namar is his grandfather."

Fudd was impressed. The girls had his full attention.

Katy took the conversation from there. "Jedediah said he was learnin' a lot about his Cherokee side. He said he felt pride for both his Cherokee and his Irish heritage."

Katy stopped walking and stared blankly into the distance. "It isn't fair how the tribes are treated." Katy felt tears welling in her eyes. She turned her head so the others wouldn't see the despair that had suddenly overtaken her. Ruben and Ellie pretended not to notice.

They continued walking down the road past the edge of town. It was about a half mile to the Fudd homestead and another mile or so to the Highlands' Ranch.

"Will you walk us home, Ruben?" asked Ellie. "I'm afraid of that nasty old mountain lion." Ellie eyed him softly; she could melt a guy's resolve with a doe-like charm if that was her intent. Fudd continued to kick the ground with the toe of his boot and looked away. Ellie had always been able to have her way with him. He liked it much more than he was willing to admit, even to himself.

"I don't think I'll have to 'cause I can see your daddy's buggy comin' this way."

The girls turned and looked in the direction of their homestead. Thunder and Lightning kicked dust into the air as they trotted toward the threesome.

Cletus Highland pulled up next to the kids and turned the horses and buggy around. Thunder and Lightning were an impressive team of horses. Thunder was a dark, chestnut-brown stallion and Lightning was a lighter brown mare with a white, bolt-shaped mark on her forehead.

"I appreciate you watchin' after my girls until I arrived, Ruben," said Cletus.

"Yes, sir, Mr. Highland," said Fudd as he kicked at the ground a bit more. The girls climbed into the buggy.

"Glad to see you up and about so quick after that snake bite. Would you like a lift to your house?"

"Naw. I'm gonna take the path to the river first and catch me a few fish."

"All right, then, son, but you watch out for that big cat."

Fudd looked up with a mischievous smile on his face and said, "Oh, I hope I do see that cat. It would make my day." It was plain to see that Ruben Fudd's close call had not diminished his confidence in himself as a woodsman.

Ellie asked if they could invite Ruben over for dinner. Cletus turned and eyed his daughter with an amused look on his face. "We'll have to see about that," he said.

Ellie wasn't sure whether that was a promising answer or not.

They all turned back to Fudd and Cletus tipped his hat. "Much obliged, Ruben. I'll be needin' some help at the ranch Tuesday and Wednesday if you are up to it. Zeb and Lester are quitting on me to join the travelin' rodeo, smack in the middle of harvest."

Katy grinned with the news and looked at her sister. Ellie took the news with a smile as well. Apparently they felt that Zeb being gone was a stroke of fortune even if it meant more work for them during the harvest.

"Yes, sir, I'll be there," said Fudd. Clete nodded in acknowledgement and snapped the reins, and Thunder and Lightning trotted on down the road.

≫—11—→
ASIDE THE JACKSON RIVER

FUDD SAT along the bank of the Jackson River. He could see where the Jackson met the Cowpasture River—the confluence of the James River. He sat down and took position just below a small set of rapids. This was his honey hole for catching smallmouth bass. The sun's rays sparkled in the ripples of the water, producing thousands of tiny points of light. Fluffy white clouds passed through a brilliant blue sky. Fudd turned his face into the sun and closed his eyes. The breeze blew lightly across his face and neck, softening the warming rays of the sun. All in all it was a great day to be alive. He enjoyed the solitude of the moment, as his mind was heavy with everything that had transpired over the last four days.

He had almost died on Tuesday. Patricia, his schoolmate, had been killed by a mountain lion that very same day. Hood had come back to Glen Wilton. Some people liked having Hood back and some people did not. The day had been chock-full of danger and controversy. Word was out about the stranger because Emmett wanted him hung for shooting Aikman. Emmett was also bad-mouthing Hood, insisting that Hood and the stranger were in on the plot together. He claimed that they had laid in wait to get the rest of the money the stranger hadn't cheated him out of earlier. Fudd didn't know Hood well, but he didn't believe it.

The fishing was a little slow that afternoon, but he still caught several good-sized smallmouth bass. As he was about to quit fishing for the day, he caught a small brown trout. He wished the trout had been a bit bigger; trout was his favorite. He tossed it back into the river, suggesting that it grow a little and then find his hook again. It was time to trek on home. He needed to get the bass cleaned up so his mom could cook them up for dinner.

»—12—→
THE SECRET PLACE

HOOD PICKED his way through the forest, following old, familiar landmarks to the secret place he hadn't laid eyes on in four years. It was the morning of Patricia's funeral, and as he walked, he was trying to decide whether or not to attend. Oliver was enjoying all the pastureland and the shelter provided by the barn, so Hood had left him behind. It was much easier to travel undetected without a mule leaving a trail of hoof-prints in the soft earth, anyway.

Hood had spent the previous two days making improvements to the barn and to the pasture fencing. The barn was becoming quite comfortable. His hands ached from cuts and blisters earned while splitting the seventeen fence rails that were needed to secure the pasture. The new axe handle he'd made had performed well. He thought back to stories of the former President Abraham Lincoln that he'd read in school. Abe had been a champion rail-splitter and wrestler as a youth. Ultimately though, it was his education, not his physical strength that set him apart and made him special.

As Hood continued to walk, his thoughts shifted to his family. He missed them terribly and knew that this errand would only add to that sense of loss. The spot he was heading to had saved the lives of what was left of his family the day his Pops was murdered. He wondered what Sequoia and Cher were doing right now. He said a quick prayer to the great Lord and Savior to protect them in his absence. He asked his forefathers for guidance. His Pops was with them now. Hood knew that one day, he too would take his place among them in the stars. This life is short, and it is a struggle.

He thought about God and the different ways the Cherokee, and other cultures, chose to worship him. It seemed to Hood that they all honored the same great being, though they gave him different names and worshipped in different ways. Growing up in the house of his father, however, had exposed him to God's written word. He wished that more of his Cherokee brothers knew about Jesus, but he understood that it was complicated.

Losing his father had forced him to grow up fast. By age eleven, he had fully understood that life is not fair. Some people are born with an advantage and some are not. Some people work for all they have, only to have it stolen by others. His father had taught him at an early age that sometimes he might have to stand alone to protect himself or those he loved. He thought of a remark his father had made when he complained about being bullied by Zeb Henry.

"If you are not being treated equal, then be equal to the occasion."

The next day, as Hood was leaving the school house, Zeb tripped him as he walked down the front steps. Zeb and his best friend, Lester, crowed with delight. Zeb was stunned when Hood sprang to his feet and let fly a mighty blow that caught him square in the nose. Blood spurted everywhere. Lester and Zeb retaliated, and Hood felt the sting of many blows, but he fought like a wild cat and stood his ground. Ultimately, Zeb chose not to physically challenge Hood anymore. He was embarrassed that Hood had fought to a standoff with the odds two-on-one. He was reduced to verbal taunts from that time on, which Hood handled with a grain of salt.

In the months that followed his Pops's murder, Hood had been filled with an inconsolable rage and hate. No one could reach him. His grandfather, Chief Namar, had devoted much of his time to Hood in those days, hoping to share the burden of his troubled heart. Time can heal many wounds, but this one was deep and bitter. Grandfather and grandson went on many walks through the forest together. At first, few words passed between the two, but with each walk they spoke a little more, and gradually Hood began to reveal that wound, which Chief Namar set to tending.

Slowly, Hood began to learn a new way of looking at the world. It was an ancient way. It was not as backward and unsophisticated as he had previously thought. His grandfather used Cherokee legends to teach him simple lessons like the virtue of patience, and how one bad decision can lead to many others. Two particular stories came cascading back into his memory.

THE LEGEND OF THE HUNGRY HUNTERS

Many years ago, a great bowman named Grey Wolf was teaching his twin sons how to hunt and feed their tribe. The women and children were hungry because food was scarce, and the men feared for the survival of those whom they loved. He explained to his sons, Eyes of Hawk and Silver Fox, that the Spirit of the Forest would feed them if they respected the balance of life of all the forest creatures. "Only take the males of a species, for the female is the giver of new life."

They split up and hunted all of the first day, but they found no game and their stomachs rumbled. The second day, Silver Fox watched as a doe and two fawns walked within range of his bow. He was hungry, but he heeded the words of Grey Wolf and he let them pass. Within the hour, a large buck followed the same path, and Silver Fox made a skillful shot.

Later that day, the doe and her fawns walked past Eyes of Hawk and he was excited. The words of his father were still in his head, but the hunger was in his stomach, so he shot the doe and the fawns ran away. Despite his disobedience, he felt his father would still be pleased because they needed to feed the tribe.

When all the hunters returned to camp, Grey Wolf was angry with Eyes of Hawk. "You have offended the Spirit of the Forest with your impatience. Now we have enough food for a feast, but we have taken from our future."

Eyes of Hawk justified his actions defiantly. "We need two deer to feed the tribe. To kill this deer was in the best interest of all those we love."

"No, my son, it is not. Now four deer will die, and we will only eat two because the fawns will not survive, nor will they grow up and have fawns of their own. That cycle of life assures the tribe's future." At that moment, they heard the yelps of the coyote pack making their kill.

THE PATHS MARKED GOOD AND EVIL

Silver Fox and Eyes of Hawk were brothers born on the same day. They grew into manhood together and were the best of friends. They walked the same path of life and enjoyed each other's companionship. One day they came to a fork in the path. One direction was marked Good and the other marked Evil.

Eyes of Hawk said, "Let us see what there is to see down this path marked Evil."

Silver Fox said, "I cannot walk down that path."

"The paths are close to one another," Eyes of Hawk noted. "If we do not like what we see, then we can cross back over to the path marked Good."

"I will not walk down that path with you, my brother," said Silver Fox.

"I am curious, so I will walk this path for a short while, and then I will cross back over to the path marked Good. I will tell you what I see."

"There is nothing along that path that will interest me," responded Silver Fox. "I will miss you if you take that path."

The brothers parted company, but they could still see each other, as the paths were nearly parallel. As they travelled further, the paths changed course, and they got further apart. Finally, Eyes of Hawk broke away from the path marked Evil and worked his way through the thick underbrush and thistle and found his brother on the path marked Good. They were happy to be together once again. Eyes of Hawk had many stories of adventure, but he was tired, and he had scars from his journey.

After walking on the path marked Good for a while, Eyes of Hawk grew restless and asked his brother to join him on the path marked Evil because there was so much to see. Once again, Silver Fox said that he could not travel that path. His heart ached as he watched his brother leave.

Eyes of Hawk found that the way back to the path marked Evil was open and wide and contained no underbrush or thistle. He was happy to see that it was an easy journey. For many moons he stayed on that path, and it took him further away from his brother and the path marked Good.

The path marked Evil eventually lost its luster and to continuously walk it became a burden. He bore many more scars from the journey. He longed to be again with his brother on the path marked Good, but he wasn't sure if he could find the way. Finally, he set off to find his brother. It was a courageous journey; often he was lost, since the underbrush and thistle were much thicker than before. The journey took many days and many nights. Along the way, Eyes of Hawk received many wounds and scars, but he finally found the path marked Good and was reunited with his brother. The brothers embraced with much joy.

For many moons, the brothers were happy. As time passed, Eyes of Hawk's scars began to heal. The pain that he felt on the path marked Evil began to fade. As he looked from the path marked Good toward the path marked Evil, a small path opened up and he could see that it was an easy journey. He again indulged himself on the path marked Evil, but the path once again lost its luster.

He reasoned that he could find his way back to the path marked Good at any time he pleased. After all, he had done so before. When he finally tried and set off for the path marked Good, he found a terrible surprise. The paths pointed in completely opposite directions, and he was lost in the forest forever.

As Hood grew older and these lessons of wisdom shaped his character, he began to more fully understand the plight of the Cherokee. He could see the fears that his grandfather had for the future of the tribe. This fear, however, was never shown in anger. When Hood expressed outrage at the injustices inflicted on the Cherokee and his desire for revenge, the Chief would calm him and explain that he could better serve his people with his mind than with his might.

"Sit with me, my son, and let us talk of the consequences of such a fight," Chief Namar would say.

Hood could still see the fire burning brightly outside of the entrance of his grandfather's tepee. Hood wanted to pace and rant, but the Chief calmly relit his peace pipe and then motioned for Hood to take a seat near him. Reluctantly, Hood did as was requested and basic logic won the day. Taking arms against the white man would be futile, and many who they cared for would die.

"Choose the path of the white man," his grandfather had said, to Hood's astonishment and disbelief. "Go to his schools. Learn his wisdom and mingle it with that of the Cherokee. And then treat your Cherokee brothers well."

His grandfather would go on, "Your fate is known only to the Great One. The path you choose is yours. But you share the same desire as every man who has ever gazed at the stars and known that there is something greater than ourselves.

"The gift of life is the greatest gift that can ever be given. This is what makes it hard to take the life of another. Do you love your neighbor or do you envy him? Do you appreciate the deer that feeds and clothes you? We are stewards over the Great One's beasts of the forest. The Great One even gives purpose to the lowly tick. The tick goes about its business. The turkey eats the tick. We eat the turkey. One day the worm will feast on the man.

"You should always ask, 'How may I please you, Great One?' Do not value another man's answer to this question over your own. His journey belongs to him and his answer may be different from yours. The Great One will tell you what to do if you take the time to listen. Reflect, don't react. Large thoughts demand to be pondered, and pondering often takes a lifetime.

His grandfather had taught him so many things—the ways of men and the ways of the forest.

Hood meditated on his grandfather's stories as he walked through the woods towards the secret place. He was having more trouble finding the entrance to the ancient cave than he expected. The opening was a small crease in the rock face, and he just couldn't seem to spot it. Finally, he noticed that a large chestnut tree had fallen and blocked the crease from view.

Time changes everything. It stops for no one.

He climbed over the thick trunk. "The blight" was killing off the chestnuts on his land too. His land. It felt funny to think of the land as his and not his Pops's. He dropped to his knees, brushed the old vines to the left and stuck his head into the entrance. The old coach lamp was right where he had left it. He pulled it out and sat on the trunk of the grand old chestnut tree. He fished into his pack and found his flint.

Once the lamp was lit, he pulled out his Bowie knife. Then, with a reflective smile, he slid it back into his sheath and pulled out his new revolver. Bears sometimes like to hibernate in this old cave, although it was still very early for that. He worked his way through the entrance. After a fifteen-foot crawl on his hands and knees, Hood came to a spot where the crevice opened up into a small cavern. The light from his lamp flickered dimly on the walls around him and he rose to his feet. As Hood reacquainted himself with his surroundings, he laughed as he realized that time hadn't changed this place a bit. Time was measured in eons here, not years.

He heard the occasional drip of water, which served as the only clock in this place of utter darkness. He could hear the bats rustling where a tunnel left the cavern and led deeper into the mountain. He had never seen all the wonders that this ancient cave had to offer. One could easily get lost in a cavern such as this.

He walked over to the corner where he had stashed all the fragments of his former life. A small pile of household goods had been toppled and scattered about on the dusty floor, probably the result of critters foraging in search of food. His Pops's favorite ceramic coffee cup had survived the fire and now lay broken against a rock. Hood fought back his first tear.

The day his Pops was killed, he and his mother and sister were reluctant to leave town without his father's body. Sheriff Green encouraged them to go because the daylight was already fading. He needed a few more hours to examine Jake's body, so he urged them to go home and return in the morning. As they approached their homestead, though, they could see the bright glow of a huge fire burning in the distance, and when they drew nearer, they could hear the hoots and hollers of the Cowboys as they ransacked the ranch. Hood led his crying mother and sister away from harm, to this secret cave, undetected. The next day they went back to the ranch to see if they could recover anything of value.

As they picked through the charred rubble, turning over logs and digging in the ashes, their tears disappeared into the sooty remains. They retrieved what they could, moving all their salvageable belongings to the cave with the help of the only surviving animal, Oliver the mule. Then they made a tough decision: they would flee and join up with the tribe. The tribe was family too, and it would protect them. They took a day to prepare for the journey and left the safety of the cave the following night. They traveled by foot and took only what they and their young mule could carry. Five days later, they were living with the tribe.

A drop of water from the cavern's ceiling hit Hood on the nose and startled him back to the present. He had gotten lost in the past and needed to turn his mind to his task. Inventory. What did he have and what did he need?

Very little had been salvaged from the house, just some ceramic dishes and a few pieces of silverware. They were scorched but useable. He saw the kettle that they used as a coffee pot. Perfect. It was made of cast iron. No wonder it had survived. He was ready to make more coffee and thought of the cup he had enjoyed with his new friend, T.R. Most of what was saved had come from either the barn or the shed. The shed was set away from the cabin and was used as a combination workshop and root cellar. It had been left untouched.

He found a set of old clothing that wouldn't fit him now, and some old clothes of his Pops's that might fit. He saw his dad's good cowboy boots, dropped to his knees and rubbed the old leather—it was dry and a bit musty. They needed a good coat of mink oil. Leaning against a rock was a burlap sack wrapped tightly around Pops's .40 caliber Winchester repeating lever action rifle. He unwrapped the gun and inspected it closely. This weapon would be in good order with a cleaning. He had the necessary tools to do it. He also had seventeen cartridges, but knew he needed more. He had tools, lanterns, kerosene and oil. A small pile of mason jars lay in a corner that could be used for canning vegetables, and many still contained food, as they had been retrieved from the root cellar. He inspected them more closely to see if the seals were still intact. They appeared to be holding.

He stood again and walked over to the strong box that was hidden in a hole under a rock. The box didn't lock, which was fine because he didn't have the key. It had survived the fire because it was hidden in a hole beneath the old cabin floorboards. Hood was willing to bet that Emmett and the Cowboys had torn the old place apart looking for gold or any other valuables before they set the cabin on fire, but they were out of luck. The gold coins were still in the box. He knew exactly where to look for it amidst the rubble. Hood, Sequoia and Cher had taken a few coins with them when they fled, but decided to leave the rest hidden in hopes of one day returning. They knew that they wouldn't need money once they joined up with the tribe. It was no grand fortune, Hood thought, raking through the coins with his fingers, but it testified to what a smart and endeavoring rancher his Pops had been.

Hood had no immediate need of money. He had survived on his skills as a woodsman for four years, with the tribe and without. Still, he considered, a horse would be a good addition to the mule if he were to stay and work the land. He pulled two gold twenty-dollar coins from the box. Forty dollars would purchase a very strong horse. He thought about Oliver and concluded that it may be best to sell him. Even if he kept him corralled in the pasture, it gave opportunity to his enemy. They could lay in wait for him to tend his mule. The thought of saying goodbye to another loved one deflated his spirit even more. A horse would be a luxury for travel but might present the same problem. He decided to ponder the thought for a while.

He missed his family so much. He had known that seeing all of their belongings would bring back a flood of memories, but he hadn't realized just how wide and deep that flood would be. His thoughts shifted to his friend, Patricia. Her family must miss her terribly now. He pulled out an extra twenty-dollar coin. He would give it to Madeline, her sister.

Hood raised the lantern once more, letting the light fall on a small, square bundle. This was the object he'd most dreaded and longed to gaze upon. His one true treasure—the picture of his family in happier times, before it had been so violently ripped apart. The picture had been taken one month before his Pops had been shot, to the date.

Hood had been making a frame for the picture in the back shed the week before the fire. Because of this, the picture had survived. He unwrapped the burlap he had used to protect it, then repositioned the lantern so he could get a better look. Tears welled in his eyes as he looked at the black and white image of his family. He remembered how happy they had been when they were all together. They had forged a comfortable existence in this small, backwoods community. He ran his fingers over the images of his father and then his mother. The feelings of loss became so overwhelming that he had to turn away. He sat in the dim lighting with his back to the framed picture and cried.

With great effort, he willed himself out of this sadness. His grief transformed into anger. He turned his attention to his reasons for returning home. His goal was to reclaim his family's land and to stand against those who opposed him. His grandfather had once told him, "The rabbit runs and will often live to see another day. When one has no other choice, it is wise to be the rabbit, but the predators will still keep coming. Look for the advantage to turn to your favor, for one day you will have to stand like a lion for your right to live." With these words echoing in his head, Hood began to clean his father's Winchester rifle and then his new pistol.

As Hood worked, he thought of what to do next. Of the many things he needed to do, he had to go to Patricia's funeral. His mind was made up now. He wanted to go. He wanted to give Madeline the twenty-dollar gold coin and say how sorry he was that she had lost Patricia. He wanted to see his old friends from school. It seemed a lifetime ago that he had been a boy in school. Almost a normal boy. He missed his former life. He had been happy. How long had it been since he had laughed with his friends? Katy could always make him laugh. Katy… she would be there. He raised the lantern again and looked around the cave. He knew he had a few bars in there somewhere.

"There they are." He had found them. Two bars of lye soap. He grabbed one of the bars and headed out of the cave toward the creek. It was time to clean up his act. Time to see some old friends.

≫─13─→
THE #2 TRAIN

HOOD WAS clean and refreshed as he walked toward Iron Gate. The bath in the cold creek water invigorated him from head to toe. The lye soap was rough on the skin, but he felt great now.

As Hood traveled, he noticed a pair of heavily armed men in the woods. One man had his nose to the ground tracking while his partner scanned for danger. They didn't notice Hood as he skirted around them to avoid detection. Even though it seemed that they were after the bounty on the mountain lion, Hood stayed clear, as he didn't want to meet anyone out in the wilderness.

In his back pouch, Hood carried the four pistols that belonged to the Cowboys. He had emptied the chambers and kept the bullets. He wasn't about to give Emmett a loaded gun. He didn't want to return them at all, but after a spirited debate with himself about tossing them into the river, he finally resolved to follow T.R.'s advice. He felt it wise to leave his new pistol in the cave until he'd taught himself how to use it. To wear a pistol implied that you could defend yourself. If you could not use it skillfully, then it made you vulnerable.

He was walking along the tracks near the river when he heard the train whistle in the distance. The train was headed in the same direction Hood was. He smiled. His ride was on the way. Hood knew he'd have to relearn the train schedule now that he was back. He laughed as he recalled how Driver 8 had teased him about his early train-hopping days. And he'd thought he'd been so slick! The engine of the train churned past him now, and he could tell it was the number two. Casey Jones was the driver of this train, and he usually drove faster than anyone. This time, though, the cars were loaded and moving slowly. Hood dashed from his hiding place alongside the tracks and grabbed onto the ladder of the coal car, just like old times.

⇒—14—→
IRON GATE

THE TOWN seemed different somehow. Everything seemed smaller and closer together. Hood was early for the funeral, so he decided that now would be a good time to go visit Sheriff Green. He would hand over the pistols and tell his side of the story.

He strolled right down the middle of Main Street. It was high noon and the day was glorious. People were everywhere, but no one seemed to take particular notice of him. He was dressed to fit into the white man's world. He was wearing his Pops's old denim Levi pants and his Pops's good boots. He had worked a little mink oil into the leather. He had on his Pops's blue shirt with ruffled sleeves and a thin vest with four buttons in the front. He wished he had a watch and chain like the one T.R. wore. He supposed that would look nice with this vest. The clothing fit him fairly well. The only tell-tale sign that he was not a typical settler was the long, wavy black hair flowing out from under his bowler hat. He was part Cherokee and, therefore, he would always be different. He had hidden his bow and arrows just outside of town. He carried his back pouch over his left shoulder. He didn't think he would need to protect himself in the middle of the day in the heart of Iron

Gate. He still had his knife, but that didn't yell "Indian" like wearing the bow and quiver would.

As he neared the center of town, he recognized an old school chum, Elizabeth Duran. Her father, Xavier, owned the Trading Post. Elizabeth was a true Southern belle, born in Atlanta. She was shy, sweet and caring, always without pretence. One would describe her as genuine.

Her father was the only member of his family to survive the burning of Atlanta by Sherman's troops. After the war, he had married his longtime sweetheart, Lisa Beatty. Elizabeth was born, and they joyously gave her a proper Southern upbringing. When Elizabeth was only five, her mother had died trying to give birth to a second child. The baby boy died as well, and all the joy they'd previously known seemed sucked from their very souls.

Xavier eventually yearned to start a new life away from the big city, so he and his daughter migrated North. They got as far as Glen Wilton and Iron Gate, Virginia. They fell in love with the harmony of the community and decided to plant some roots here.

Elizabeth recognized Hood immediately, ran up to him, and gave him a great big hug. Elizabeth wasn't quite as young or shy as he had remembered, and she smelled slightly of perfume. Hood wasn't quite sure how to respond! Blushing, he backed away from the embrace. Elizabeth enjoyed Hood's discomfort as if it were a compliment, but then she skillfully started the conversation to put him at ease.

"Jedediah, Jedediah, Jedediah," she cried. "It's so good to see you! The rumors have been flying around town that your were back. My goodness, you can sure make a big splash in a little pond!"

Hood smiled sheepishly and said, "I didn't really mean to make any waves. I kinda like it better when no one really notices me."

Elizabeth frowned, not sure if Hood had meant her, and Hood quickly added, "I'm really glad to see you, though."

Her face brightened again.

"Word is out that you helped gun down one of Emmett's Cowboys," said Elizabeth.

"That's not how it happened at all," said Hood, his face growing somber. "I didn't shoot anyone. I'm on my way to tell the Sheriff about it now."

They started walking toward the Trading Post and the Sheriff's office beyond. Elizabeth grabbed Hood by the elbow and wrapped her arm through his. The years of his absence seemed to disappear as she strolled along beside him, confident and smiling. She had changed quite a bit in four years, but she treated him as an old friend and not like a savage who had been run out of town. Hood wasn't sure who was escorting whom, but he began to take pleasure in the moment.

"Everyone is meeting over at the school at two o'clock for the funeral. Did you hear about poor Patricia?" Her eyes began to mist and she produced a lacy handkerchief and blotted them.

"Yeah," said Hood. "The Doc told me."

"Well, Miss Summers is going to have cookies and cider, and then Mr. Highland is going to give us a hayride over to the church. It's so sad. I can't believe that nasty old mountain cat killed poor Patricia. I've never been so afraid of the woods before." Her smile vanished and she dabbed at her eyes once again. "Ruben would be dead too if you hadn't shown up when you did. Oh, say you will come over to the school. Everyone will want to see you."

They stopped in front of the Trading Post. Hood said he'd try to make it to the school and that he was planning on being at the funeral.

Elizabeth said farewell with a warning, "You watch out for Emmett Stone. Word is he's pretty mad at you. He says he's gunnin' for you and that stranger."

SHERIFF GREEN

SHERIFF GREEN had always liked the Hood family, and it was sad that they were no longer intact. Jake and Sequoia Hood had been very friendly to the community. They had attended the Iron Gate Baptist Church every Sunday, and those that got to know Sequoia and the kids had accepted them easily. Sequoia rarely came to town alone, though; she was wise enough to realize that some folks could never accept an Indian living among them. Because of his love for Sequoia and her family, this type of prejudice had driven Jake to fight against the removal of the tribes from their lands. He used any legal means possible to draw attention to the politicians who unfairly destroyed their lifestyle. As Sheriff, Green could respect the civilized way that Jake had chosen to fight.

The Sheriff closed the paper he was reading and took another sip of coffee. It was cold. He set the cup back down on his desk. What was he going to do? The mountain lion had killed four people in his jurisdiction and plenty of livestock. Emmett and the Cowboys were hanging around again and that was never good. Everyone took what Emmett had to say about the incident with a grain of salt, but there was still a shooting to investigate. He was now bound by duty, even if Artimus Aikman was a trouble-causin' scallywag. Things were getting pretty hectic in his peaceful little community. The Lord was held in high regard on Sundays, but there were six other days to the week. At least all the jail cells were empty. He would have to find Hood soon and hear his side of the story.

The bell above his front door jangled and the Sheriff looked up. There stood Jedediah Hood.

"Well, hello there, Mr. Hood."

Hood dipped his head by way of hello. This was the second time he'd been called "Mister," but he didn't enjoy it as much this time.

"It seems you were unable to come home quietly," remarked Sheriff Green.

"I didn't mean to cause no fuss, Sheriff," Hood said defensively.

"Well, that was a fine thing, getting Ruben to the doctor like you did. Doc says that Ruben would have probably died out there in the wilderness so far away from help if you hadn't happened along. This town is grateful for your heroic actions."

Hood didn't know what to say. He was afraid he might end up behind bars by coming here. This was not the welcome he'd expected.

"Yes, sir," was all he could manage to say.

"Seems you ran into a little trouble for all your efforts, though," the Sheriff said, somewhat reservedly.

"Yes, sir," Hood responded, again thinking that retribution was on its way. He thought he'd better explain. "Emmett and those Cowboys ambushed me on my way out of town from the Doc's office. I was in a heap of trouble 'til T.R. stepped in to my defense."

"T.R., eh?" said the Sheriff. "Tell me about this T.R. fellow."

"T.R. is a man from New York City who came down here to hunt that killer mountain lion."

"Ah, I see. A bounty hunter, this rider."

"Not really, Sheriff. I don't think he's doin' it for the money."

"No? Then why do you suppose he's doin' it?"

"'Cause the lion kills people," Hood said, reflectively. "T.R.'s a good man."

"Well, Emmett said that rider gunned down one Artimus Aikman in cold blood. He had no cause."

"That ain't true, Sheriff. Aikman drew on him first. T.R. tried to stop those boys without shootin'. They had their guns trained on me and he made 'em drop 'em. That Cowboy had a second gun and he tried to shoot T. R. when he was dealing with Emmett."

"I figured those rough-and-tumble Cowboys had started the whole thing," said the Sheriff.

"T.R. said he was going to come by and see you," Hood said. "I brought in their guns." Hood removed the pack from his back and laid the four guns on the Sheriff's desk.

"Well, it looks like those roughshods ran into a rougher rider."

"T.R. told me I should bring these guns to you and tell my side of the story. I'd a probably thrown them in the river. I don't want to give ol' Emmett a gun so he can shoot me with it."

"This T.R. feller has given you some good advice. I look forward to speaking with him, but these guns are the lawful property of those Cowboys, so it's my duty to see that they are returned. I can, however, turn them over to the circuit court judge instead of giving them directly to Emmett. That might take awhile and cause Emmett a little fuss to get 'em back."

The Sheriff winked at Hood, walked around the desk and offered Hood his hand. When Hood accepted the handshake, he seemed relieved. "Most folks in this town liked your family. I'm one of them. It pains me to know what you've been through. Are your mom and sister well?"

"Yeah," said Hood. "They're with the tribe."

"I know there are some folks around here that will give you trouble," said the Sheriff.

"Not just trouble, Sheriff. Those Cowboys killed my Pops. They burned down my house. They want to kill me just for sport. Emmett ain't never gonna' leave me be. I'm tired of hiding. I'm tired of him making me feel like I ain't human." Hood could feel his hand twitch and come to rest on his knife. "I'm here to reclaim my Pops's land and I expect that Emmett ain't gonna' like it. I'll be watching my back, though, because I know already that he's a back-shooter."

"I wish we could have proved it, Jedediah, that he had shot Jake like that. There just weren't any witnesses."

They both nodded with tight, grim lips. Emmett had gotten away with murder.

⟫—16—→
THE TRADING POST

HOOD DECIDED to visit the Trading Post next. He wanted more cartridges for his Winchester rifle, the gun that he knew how to use and use well. He also wanted to ask about some horses, even if he did not intend to purchase one right away.

The Trading Post was bustling with Saturday afternoon activity. Hood didn't see Elizabeth about, but her father, Xavier, recognized him immediately.

"Well, well, well. If you leave a door open then there is no tellin' what will come through it!" Xavier's exclamation was delivered in such a friendly manner that Hood knew that no insult was intended. Xavier Duran, although hardened by life, still retained much of his Southern charm and wit.

"It appears that you have become a man during your absence," Xavier said, coming from behind the counter and unabashedly looking Hood over, head to toe. "Yes, it is not the boy, but the man that stands before me now."

Hood felt his ears growing hot under the approving gaze. Xavier may not have felt abashed, but Hood was starting to.

Other men in the Trading Post started to take note of Hood's presence. Linwood McCoy was there with his four sons and three of his nephews. None of them had ever gotten along with the Hoods. In fact, they seemed to feud with just about everyone but the Henry clan. Birds of a feather flock together. Lester McCoy was Linwood's third son and about a year older than Hood. He was also Zeb Henry's best friend. He and Zeb even dropped out of school the same day, but Hood didn't know that and wouldn't have cared if he did.

"He don't look much like a man if you was to ask me," goaded Lester.

"*I* didn't ask you," replied Hood. "Did you ask him, Mister Duran?"

"I reckon I didn't, Mr. Hood," Xavier said with a chuckle. "It really takes a man to know a man."

Lester seemed to know well enough that matching wits was not his strong suit. His older brother, Chester, though, was ready to pick up the slack. With a venomous sneer he spat out, "You will never be anything but a half-breed as long as you live."

The oldest—and by far the dumbest—son, Fester, decided to take his shot as well: "Yeah, Half-Breed."

Hood just shook his head at the lot of them and turned his back. Hester, the youngest son, was in second grade and still went to school. He secretly idolized Fudd and knew that it was Hood who had saved him. "Why don't you guys like him, Fester? He saved Ruben when he got snake bit."

Linwood said, "Shut up, boy," and smacked his son on the back of the head with his open palm.

The boy smiled sheepishly at Hood and Xavier as if this were a very common occurrence.

Hood and Xavier watched as the McCoy clan made their way out of the Trading Post and went on about their business.

Hood turned around to once again face Xavier. "There may be hope for that lot yet."

Xavier chuckled and said, "No doubt, the young one is the pick of the litter."

They both turned toward the front door again, since they could hear the McCoy clan still bickering out in the street.

"What can I do for you, Jedediah?" Xavier asked.

"I would like some shells for a .40 caliber Winchester."

Xavier nodded his approval and went back around the counter. "I have nine boxes. How many would you like?"

Hood realized that he had no idea what they cost, so he asked.

"Four bits a box."

"I'll take six." Hood handed Xavier a twenty-dollar gold piece. Xavier made change and gave him seventeen dollars in paper money. Hood inspected the bills curiously, as he had not dealt with money very often. He was more accustomed to bartering for his goods. He smiled at Xavier and stuffed the wad of cash into his denim pants. "I could use a flannel shirt and a bandanna. And I would really like some coffee."

Xavier escorted Hood to another corner of the store and they took care of their business.

Hood decided he liked shopping. He put on his new green flannel shirt and red polka dot bandanna and stuffed his blue shirt, vest, coffee and bullets into his back pouch. As he was about to leave, he inquired about the best man to talk to about getting a horse.

"Clete Highland would be your best bet there."

Hood thanked Xavier for his kindness and started for the door. Just then, in through the door came Rigger with a roll of beaver pelts under his arm.

"Hey there, boy!" he called out. Hood felt he had been put back in his place. Rigger was a huge man and everyone felt small around him. His beard held just a tint of red to it even though his hair was brown. Hood took note of the streak of grey coming down from Rigger's chin.

Rigger extended his free hand for Hood to shake and crushed his hand in the process. "This boy ain't cuttin' into my beaver market is he, Xavier? I know he's about the second best woodsman out there." He grabbed Hood's shoulder at the collarbone and gave him a good, friendly shake. It hurt a little, but Hood wouldn't let it show.

"How about I leave the beaver for you and I'll bring in the buckskins," Hood replied.

Xavier looked at Hood earnestly and stated, "Jedediah, you bring me those buckskins and we can do us some business."

Hood felt a touch of excitement at the prospect and said, "I reckon I better do that then."

Rigger threw his beaver pelts on the counter. "Good. I'm glad we got that settled. I need five pounds of salt and three new traps. Git me some .40 caliber bullets as well."

"Only three boxes left." Xavier winked at Hood.

"I'll take 'em all."

Hood said that he'd best be getting along, and all said their farewells. Hood left the Trading Post feeling very good about the visit. He had always liked the Trading Post. As he stepped back into the brightness of the afternoon sun, he swung his pack onto his left shoulder. His new shirt felt stiff and clean, and he headed on down the dusty road.

⫸—17—→
BACK TO SCHOOL

BUDDY WAS the first to notice Hood's presence as he stood at the far edge of the schoolyard, watching the preparations. The girls were standing together in one group and the boys together in another. Miss Summers was putting cider and cookies on a picnic table. Mr. Highland was watering his horses as they stood attached to a wagon full of hay. Buddy's head turned into the wind and he made out Hood in an instant. He trotted over to Hood, wagging his tail as he approached. He had known it was Hood's smell even after all the lye soap. Hood knelt down and rubbed Buddy behind the ears.

Fudd was the first to walk over to where Hood and Buddy were. "I was hoping to see you again," he said as he grabbed Hood by the shoulders and shook him heartily. "Then again, I was hoping to see anyone again!" The two boys laughed as the groups of boys and girls converged on them. The questions started flying excitedly from all directions. Hood wasn't used to so much attention, or at least not to so much positive attention.

Miss Summers approached the gathering shortly thereafter. "I do declare! It's Jedediah Hood," she announced with a bright smile. She walked alongside Hood and Fudd as she ushered the kids over to the picnic table for the meal to begin. "It sure is nice to see you back at school, Jedediah. Are you just visiting or are you back for awhile?"

"I hope to be back for good," said Hood.

"Well, if you do stick around, then I'll expect you at eight o'clock on Monday morning at the beginning of next session." She smiled and Hood felt the warmth of belonging somewhere. Could it be this easy to pick up the pieces of his shattered life?

As they approached the picnic table, Hood's eyes met those of Katy Highland. She had not walked over with the other kids. She was four years older now—tall, thin, with flowing dirty-blond hair half way down her back. Her white and blue flowered sundress brushed her ankles. She was wearing short dress boots that looked to be good for horseback riding. Her smile melted him completely. She was more beautiful than he remembered, and he remembered. Hood's tongue felt thick in his mouth. This moment seemed harder than dragging Fudd to the doctor.

"Hey there, stranger," Katy greeted him, taking the lead in the conversation.

"I guess I'm back in town," Hood managed to say.

Katy poured two cups of cider and handed one to Hood. "I guess you are," she said with a demure look as she took a sip.

Hood felt caught in a spell. He wanted to run, but he didn't dare. Ellie, Katy's twin sister, joined the conversation. She wore a white and yellow flowered dress. They never wore the exact same outfit. She gave Hood a playful shove. The spell was broken.

"You need to answer some questions, young man," stated Ellie as she put her hands on her hips. "Everyone wants to know if Sequoia and Cher are okay."

Hood nodded.

"Everyone also wants to know what you're gonna do about Emmett and the Cowboys."

Hood shrugged.

"And Katy wants to know if you are coming back to school."

Hood and Katy both turned red and all the old friends laughed. Ellie had never been one for subtleties.

The reunion was going well. Hood had missed the feeling of his school and the Glen Wilton community for so long. It suddenly dawned on him just how important it all was to him. The tribe was a community of outcasts in their own nation. He had heard it from his elders, but he was just beginning to realize it for himself. There was no future for him there with the tribe. His future was tied to the legacy his father had left him: the white man's universe, their amazing inventions, their dynamic society and their prejudice and cruelty. As he looked around at the smiling faces of his former classmates, Hood felt for the first time in years that this was where he belonged. Then, suddenly, another face flashed to mind—Emmett's face—and it wasn't smiling. Hood swallowed hard. He mustn't forget that not everyone shared his opinion.

≫─18─→
THE HAYRIDE

"TIME TO GO!" yelled Hr. Highland. "Load 'em up!" The kids all piled into the wagon.

"Could you scoot over a little, Jedediah?" Lump tapped the side of Hood's leg and then scrunched between Hood and Katy and plopped down. He had a *Roanoke Times* from yesterday that his father had given him. He displayed it proudly for all the kids to see, but it was Katy he wanted to impress.

Lenny Stump was fourteen, smart, plump and a little shy. He couldn't remember not having a crush on Katy Highland. The kids all called him Lump, even his friends. Kids could be so cruel and not even realize it. He hated his nickname, though he rarely let it show. If he did, it usually just made things worse. Katy had always called him Leonard or Lenny, and she had stuck up for him on more than one occasion. She had a powerful personality, kind of like Miss Summers. When she got her dander up, people just naturally took a step back. Lenny knew deep down that he would never be more than a dear friend to Katy, but still, he didn't want to give up hope. At least as a dear friend he got to be near her. The way she was looking at Hood was driving him crazy, though.

She had never looked at him like that, and it was torture.

There were eleven students in the back of the hay wagon. Miss Summers rode in the front with Mr. Highland. Cletus Highland was wearing his pistol and had a rifle on a side mount. The only other people with weapons were Ruben, with his trusty Hawkins rifle and Jedediah, with his knife, bow and a quiver full of arrows. He had retrieved them from their hiding spot when he left the main part of town to come over to the school. Both boys laid their weapons down in the hay. As the wagon pulled away from the school, Buddy shot out in the lead.

Lenny laid the paper in Katy's lap and smiled. "Why, thank you, Lenny," said Katy.

"Wow, this is yesterday's paper from Roanoke. How did you get it so quickly?"

Lenny Stump beamed with pride. "My daddy rode in from Fincastle last night, and they get the *Roanoke Times* the same day there." The kids all seemed impressed.

Roanoke was the up and coming city of the mountain region. Two years ago, in 1886, the town of Big Lick had renamed itself the city of Roanoke. It seemed kind of odd to Hood that the Indian tribes got so little respect from the settlers until it came time to name something. Then, all of a sudden, an Indian name implied prestige.

Jeannie Cleary chimed in, "We can't all see it. Katy, will you read it out loud to us?" Everyone was nodding with excitement at the prospect of current news.

Katy said, "Of course," and began to scan the paper. "Here is one about that mountain lion." She began to read:

"Mountain Lion Continues Its Reign of Terror. This bold and fearless mountain lion has gripped the small communities of Glen Wilton and Iron Gate in its reign of terror. Her first human victim was taken almost five months ago. Yes, we did refer to the big cat as a female.

"Yesterday's victim was a goat owned by Hook Dunbar. Here is what Mr. Dunbar had to say: 'I seen that cougar jump out of its crouch and pounce

on my Billy goat. By the time I got my rifle, she was almost to the wood's edge, carrying old Billy by the neck. The cat walked directly away from me, so I could tell it didn't have any male parts. Then, she was in the woods and I had no shot.'

"This man-eating lion has claimed four human lives and an untold number of livestock. The latest human victim was Patricia Gordon, a girl of just fourteen years. The community of Glen Wilton wails in pain as they prepare to bury this child tomorrow at Iron Gate Baptist Church.

"'How long will this beast haunt us?' That's what Jeannie Cleary wants to know."

Everyone in the cart turned and looked at Jeannie. She had gotten a quote in the *Roanoke Times*. Everyone was impressed.

"'How do you kill a ghost?' That's what William Abbott wants to know.

"'Does the mountain lion have a litter of kits out there somewhere?' That's what Genevieve Bernsley wants to know.

"What we do know is the bounty has gone up again and again, and that brings the total to $900. The Roanoke Times would like to add $100, so now we have the largest bounty ever on a killer animal. Hopefully, the $1,000 bounty will help answer all these fearful questions."

Katy looked up from the paper. Everybody's eyes were wide with astonishment. Even Mr. Highland seemed gripped by the attention their little community was receiving.

"You kids really need to stay out of the woods until that mountain lion gets killed," admonished Miss Summers. "This bounty is going to bring even more hunters to our area. Trigger-happy hunters might be just as dangerous as the mountain lion." The students nodded their heads in acknowledgement.

As Katy began flipping through the rest of the paper, everyone crowded their heads together to see. There was an advertisement for the famous amazing elixir, Breckenridge Brew, from Colorado. It claimed to cure everything from warts to cancer. People were skeptical of the claim, but they sure did like the brew's taste and effect.

There was an article about the two presidential candidates. The election was three short weeks away and had dominated the recent news. It was beginning to look like Benjamin Harrison might thwart President Grover Cleveland's bid for re-election.

"Can you believe they are talking about Glen Wilton in the *Roanoke Times?*" asked Elizabeth with awe in her voice.

"They're talking about that cat in the *New York Times*, too," said Hood. "I have a new friend who came down from New York City to hunt that mountain lion down."

"Another man running through the woods with a gun, it would appear," said Miss Summers as she eavesdropped on her students' conversation.

Even though the fear was very real, the excitement was palpable, too. They loved getting news from across the country and the territories, but they had rarely been a part of it.

>>—19—→
FUNERAL FOR A FRIEND

THE CHURCH was packed to the point of standing room only. As Preacher Tuck surveyed the crowd, he noted many faces that didn't usually show up on Sunday. The death of a child brought out the most basic fear in any caring parent. There, in the front row, grieving, sat the Gordon family. Out of all of Tuck's parishioners, they probably attended church most regularly. The family looked incomplete as they huddled together without the presence of Patricia. Preacher Tuck could see the hollow look on Fletch's face as he stared at the small, closed coffin in the front of the church. His wife, Millie, had her face buried into his chest under his left arm, and Madeline had her face buried under his right.

"A parent should never have to bury a child," began Preacher Tuck. "Isn't that what everyone is thinking? I'm sure that Fletch and Millie Gordon would gladly trade places with Patricia this very moment. God's ways are often hard for us to understand. He has earthly plans for Fletch, Millie and all of us that are not yet complete. For reasons unknown to us, however, his plan for Patricia is now complete. The Lord has called Patricia to dwell in his glory. Let us be happy for Patricia instead of sad. Let us celebrate the joyful life of Patricia, even though we will miss her presence. Her spirit lives on. Let us take comfort that the Lord will love and keep us all."

Preacher Tuck quoted Psalm 23. The congregation sang "Amazing Grace" and "On Jordon's Stormy Banks I Stand."

After the burial, the students approached the Gordon family. Preacher Tuck's good words had uplifted the family somewhat and they began thanking everyone for coming. Madeline asked her father if she could talk with her friends for a while and Fletch said that it would be fine.

She hugged them all, one by one. When she got to Hood, she registered mild surprise. "Oh, I didn't realize you were back." She looked into his eyes and they both felt the kindred spirit of loss. There was nothing that needed to be said. She hugged him tightly and he hugged her back.

"I wish there was something I could do," he whispered in her ear.

"There is," Madeline whispered back. "Kill that damned cat."

They pulled out of their embrace and held hands for a few seconds. Hood nodded to her in acknowledgement and then Madeline moved on and hugged the next person in line. "Thank you, Lenny, for coming. Patricia really liked you."

After the formalities of the funeral were over, everyone sat in a group under a tree near the back of the church. They cheered each other up and laughed at silly things. Life began to seem livable again. Hope crept back into everyone's hearts.

As the crowd began to disperse, Hood was approached by his Pops's best friend, Lawrence 'Larry' Stewart, the town lawyer. He practiced all forms of law, from trials to last wills. Sheriff Green had informed Larry that Hood was back in town, and Larry was looking forward to speaking to him on both a personal and professional basis.

"It's good to see you Jedediah," Larry began. "You remind me quite a bit of your father."

Hood smiled appreciatively and nodded his head.

"Looks like you're sportin' Sequoia's hair though!" Larry laughed.

"Yes, sir, I believe I am," Hood responded with a smile.

"Your father entrusted me with some papers long ago that I think we should talk about. Can you come by my office?"

"Any time you please," Hood stated emphatically.

"Now would be fine, if that works for you. We can walk together."

"Yes, sir, I'd like that, if you could give me a few minutes to say goodbye to my friends."

Larry nodded in response.

Hood approached the Gordon family once again and placed the gold coin in Madeline's hand. "If this could be put toward a headstone for Patricia, then I'd like to help."

The whole family was touched by his kindness and Fletch said, "Thank you son, but that's not really necessary." Hood closed Madeline's fingers around the coin and turned to leave.

"Thank you, Jedediah, I'm glad you're back," said Madeline as he walked away.

The sense of loss was back in his heart. The emotional swings of the day were making him feel exhausted. Hood grabbed his bow from the back of the hay wagon and started to leave with Larry. As they turned toward Larry's office, Fudd ran up alongside of Hood and asked if he could find him tomorrow. "Maybe we could go huntin' or fishin' or somethin'," he suggested.

Hood lit up at the prospect, "Sure thing!" and he turned to catch up with Larry. Hood jogged a few steps and then turned back around and grinned. "Let's meet where you got snake bit, at noon."

Fudd laughed, "Royal!"

≫—20—→
HAYRIDE BACK TO GLEN WILTON

THE REST of Miss Summers's students loaded back into the hay wagon. Thunder and Lightning trotted down the old road, bringing the group back to Glen Wilton from Iron Gate. There wasn't nearly the same level of chatter on the way back as everyone reflected on the funeral of their friend.

As they neared the old school house, they saw a group of riders standing in the road. Five riders. Fudd felt a chill go up his spine. It was Emmett and the Cowboys. Cletus pulled gently back on the reins and slowed the horses down. He glanced at his rifle, but thought it best not to make a show of force. The Cowboys rode slowly toward them, Emmett in the lead.

"Looks like you folks had a big day in Iron Gate," Emmett said as they pulled up alongside the wagon. He flashed his evil grin and his gold front teeth. Thunder whinnied loudly and nervously danced in place. The tension was so thick that even the horses could feel it. Buddy was at full alert but made no growls as he circled the wagon and riders.

Mr. Highland tugged lightly at the reins and said, "Eeeasy Thunder." Then he turned a cold expression to Emmett and said, "There isn't much joy in burying a child."

Emmett eyed the kids in the back of the wagon, his gaze moving from one to the next, as though searching for something. Fudd gripped his rifle with his thumb on the hammer and his finger by the trigger. The rifle remained concealed under the hay.

"Is there something we can do for you, Emmett? If not, then I'd like for you to let us pass."

"You can be on your way, Cletus. Me and the boys are just out doin' a little huntin'."

"Yeah," said Lazarus. "These woods are a might dangerous."

The Cowboys laughed.

"It's always a pleasure to see you, Miss Summers." Emmett flashed his teeth and tipped his hat.

Miss Summers said nothing. She just looked straight ahead and made eye contact with no one. The Cowboys laughed again.

Cletus had an urge to smash in Emmett's gold front teeth and give the gold to the church, but he thought better of it. He cracked the reins and shouldered Thunder and Lightning on past the Cowboys.

"Hope to see ya real soon, Miss Summers," Emmett said over his shoulder as they squeezed on by. One of the Cowboys let out a crowing call and they all laughed again before kicking up some dust and heading on toward Iron Gate.

"That man could give a skunk the willy-nillies," Miss Summers finally said in a quiet voice.

"Without a doubt," Clete responded, and he turned to check on the kids.

Elizabeth looked slightly pale and a little shaky. One of the other boys, Eric Pickett, had tears in his eyes but was determined not to cry. Katy and Ellie and Lump looked wide-eyed but not quite to the point of tears.

Fudd looked mad.

"It's all over now," said Mr. Highland in an effort to calm everyone down.

"They were looking for Hood. That's what they were huntin'," stated Fudd.

"I do believe you're right, Ruben," said Mr. Highland. "I think we better let Sheriff Green know about this little run-in. Hopefully, there's something he can do. I'm gonna drop all you kids off at your homes instead of the school. I want to have a word with your parents. Those Cowboys will be back and they are a danger to Jedediah Hood and anyone who is with him." Protests arose from the group, but Mr. Highland continued, "I know you are all fond of Jedediah, and I fancy him as well, but he has some deadly enemies. This community has already lost four people, and among them, one child. I do not care to see anyone else get injured."

Katy cried quietly in the rear of the wagon. It was so unfair, what Jedediah had to endure. He had just returned and she felt like he was almost gone again. Ellie moved next to Katy and hugged her older sister. She sensed the turmoil in Katy's heart. Hardly another word was spoken. The only other sounds were the clippity-clop of Thunder and Lightning's hooves on the old road and an occasional sniffle. Everyone was quiet again.

⟫—21—→
LOCAL HISTORY

THE WILDERNESS Road of Virginia had seen heavy traffic from 1775 to 1810. Three hundred thousand settlers and their families used the route, which served as a corridor between the Blue Ridge and Allegheny Mountains, snaking its way down the middle of the Shenandoah Valley. Many of the settlers fell in love with the scenic beauty of the valley and chose to go no further. By 1888, most of the native Indian tribes had been run off, disbanded or placed in settlements called reservations. Many tried to assimilate into the New World that was thrust upon them. How strange that the native population had to fit into the settlers' world instead of the other way around.

The natives that remained were often treated with scorn and disdain. They were nothing more than "savages" in the minds of most settlers. The murder of an Indian was no more immoral than killing a coyote. The Indian was of a sub-human standard.

Sequoia and her Cherokee tribe had lived in a small farming community on the west side of the Allegheny Mountains. They were the northernmost tribe of the Cherokee nation. They had been somewhat protected from the onslaught of settlers, as they were separated by thirty miles and the peaks of the mountains. The movement of people went primarily through the Shenandoah Valley. Eventually, though, some settlers did cross the Allegheny mountains and come to the Glen Wilton area, but in lesser numbers. This unique group of settlers and the local Cherokee, Monacan and Iroquois tribes chose to get along and coexist.

Not long after they met, Jake Hood and Sequoia fell in love. Most people living in the immediate vicinity didn't seem to mind. Glen Wilton was a small oasis of happiness and quiet acceptance, a small pocket of land hardly influenced by the world around it. Although it rested only three miles down river from Iron Gate, the Glen Wilton community of settlers had stronger ties to the tribal communities that had always lived there.

Change, however, is constant and inevitable. Glen Wilton's neighboring towns—Iron Gate and Clifton Forge—grew in leaps and bounds, a pace much faster than tiny Glen Wilton could muster. Iron Gate, sitting boldly next to the confluence of the Jackson and Cowpasture Rivers, which forms the James River, drew hundreds of people, and Clifton Forge, being a C&O railroad hub, drew thousands.

With more people came more ways of thinking. As the population of Iron Gate grew with new settlers, attitudes began to shift. People felt discomfort at allowing a "savage people" to live so close to what the settlers perceived as *their* land. Eventually, the Cherokee became unwelcome guests on their own land, even as the community of Glen Wilton spoke out on their behalf.

Jake Hood led Glen Wilton's effort, speaking out in the local area as well as in larger political forums in Fincastle and Roanoke. His marriage to Sequoia became a target of ridicule and a widespread symbol of betrayal to those who harbored hate in their hearts.

⟫—22—→
LARRY'S OFFICE

AS HOOD and Larry walked to Larry's office, they passed by the Dew Drop Inn and the Trading Post. Zeb Henry stumbled out of the saloon doors. He was eighteen years old now, and looking strong and fit. He was also packing a side arm. At the moment, he seemed to be practicing at taking over his dad's spot as town drunk.

He beamed with sadistic pleasure when he saw Hood on the street and launched into a taunting, barking sound. He did this to remind Hood that he was a half-breed mutt. His father, Shank Henry, wobbled out of the bar a few moments later, pointed at Hood with his finger, and roared with laughter. "You can dress him up but he's still just a half-breed." Shank laughed so hard at his own joke that he doubled over and fell on his butt. Zeb lost his footing and then plopped down next to his father. Both Henrys were laughing to the point of hysterics.

Larry and Hood just continued to walk on by. These two idiots were too wasted to be a threat to anyone but themselves.

As they approached Larry's office, the conversation turned back to Jake Hood. "Your father and I dabbled in politics with regards to fair treatment and legal rights for the native population," Larry informed

Hood. "Jake and I made more than a few trips down to Roanoke to lobby on their behalf. For the most part, the political establishment has tried to ignore the suffering of the local tribes. They like having the tribes packaged into neat little reservations.

"Your father," he continued, "had been very outspoken with regard to the sub-human treatment afforded to these people by our government. He ruffled many feathers, but also stirred debate as to the legal rights of the tribes. Because he was succeeding in helping the tribes politically, he gained enemies. I believe this is what ultimately led to his death."

Hood listened to Larry intently, surprise and pride mounting inside him. It was the first time he had heard anyone speak of his father in this way. "I had no idea he was doing all these things. He never said a word."

"I'm sure he didn't want to worry you. You were young. Political change is slow and painful. He was working to build a better world for you, Cher and Sequoia. You were eleven years old when he was killed. All this political stuff would have been a bit much for you at that age."

They had arrived at Larry's office and were standing out front at the base of the porch steps. "Why don't we go inside?" said Larry. "I have a letter for you from your father." Hood's heart skipped a beat at these words.

"A letter from Pops? How is that possible?" he thought to himself as he stepped over the wooden threshold.

Larry's office conveyed an unmistakable feeling of power. The dark paneling and shelves along the wall were neatly lined with law books. The room itself was very spacious. Larry's big desk sat near a large picture window, and an overstuffed chair sat behind the desk with the window to its back. Hood walked over to where a painting of the scales of Justice hung on the wall. Larry motioned for Hood to sit in the chair behind the desk. Hood hesitated, taking one last long look at the painting before doing as he was asked. Larry walked over to a wall safe and pulled a key from the belly pocket of his vest.

Larry reached into the safe and pulled out a small bundle of letters bound by a string. After closing the safe, he laid the packet on the desk, untied the string and handed Hood one of the letters.

"Your dad entrusted me with three letters: one for you, one for Sequoia and one for Cher. Also, I have the deed to your family land and your father's Last Will and Testament. The letter in your hand is the one your father intended for you. If you prefer, I can read it to you."

"I'm a good reader," said Hood, "I'll read it myself." ·

Larry smiled and gave Hood a nod. "I'll get a fire started in the wood stove and knock the chill out of this room." He rubbed his hands together and then warmed them with his breath as he walked over to the stove.

Hood watched for a moment as Larry began his chore. Then he returned his attention to the letter in his hand. His hands trembled a little with excitement as he started to read:

Dear Jedediah,

If you are reading this letter, then I have been called to be with the Lord. I want you to know how proud I am of you. A man could have no more love for his family than I have for you, Sequoia and Cher. My only regret is that I cannot grow old with Sequoia by my side and watch you and Cher become a fine young man and woman. I now wait with your forefathers in the sky to give meaningful wisdom to a strong young man as he grows stronger.

My first words to you from the sky are to trust and love the Lord. Do not blame Him for my death or the plight of the Cherokee.

Second, be ever vigilant in the protection of your mother and sister from those who would see them as less than they are. They will need a champion, as will others who you hold dear to your heart.

Third, find a little spot in this world and make it your own. Treat your neighbors kindly and give them the opportunity to do the same.

Embrace your destiny as it is revealed to you. Enjoy your journey through life. Choose to live with a heart that exults in what is beautiful and good.

Larry has the deed to our property in his possession. He has always been a true friend and is a man you can trust. When you turn sixteen, the land will become yours. Leave the deed with Larry. He can, and will, protect your rights of ownership.

You are aware of the location of the strong box hidden in the cabin. Be frugal with money. It is a means to an end and has no real value on its own. Larry also has control of some of my other assets. Larry will explain to you about my Last Will and Testament and how I think the money should be used. Once you are sixteen, the final choices will be yours, but please try to use the money wisely and retain a fair share for Sequoia and Cher.

Life is a struggle for everything and everyone who ever walks this earth. I fear that it will be a very tough struggle for you. Never be ashamed of who you are. I realize that you will always have to face men who are against you. It seems to be the nature of man to show prejudice against those that are not of a similar kind. Do not judge humanity by these people. If you keep your eyes open, you will find people of good character. Just as you must open your eyes and your mind to understand the forest, so you must do to understand the variety of the ways of men. Look for men of noble heart and make them your friends. Always remember to be aware of those less fortunate than yourself. Kindness seems to be a part of your nature, and I am truly thankful for that. Don't let a hard world take that away from you.

I close this letter in prayer that you will always walk with the Lord. In Him, you will live long and prosper.

Your loving Father,
Jake Hood

As Hood finished reading the letter, he felt a surge of pride for the man his father had been. He didn't bother hiding the tears in his eyes as he stared down at the familiar handwriting. Things had seemed so uncertain since his Pops had died, but now he was reaching out and showing Hood the way. Hood reread the letter several times. It seemed like an eternity before he could bring himself to fold it and tuck it away.

Larry sat with Hood and they talked of things that Jake had said and done. They shared stories of happy and sad times alike. As their reminiscing drew to a close, Hood confessed to Larry the bitter emotions he'd been harboring.

"I sometimes blame the Judge and the legal system because I know that it was Emmett that killed Pops," Hood said, stoically. "I know it, Sheriff Green knows it, heck, the Judge probably knows it. Yet, Emmett walked out of that court room a free man." Hood approached and pointed at Larry's painting of the scales. "That scale is fully tipped toward evil in my family's case."

Larry placed his hands on Hood's shoulders and looked directly into Hood's haunted eyes. "The law of the land is imperfect, I do agree. Strides are always being made to improve it. Your father fought to balance that scale, and I fight to balance that scale every day."

"It's not enough!" exclaimed Hood, his voice quivering. "Something more has to be done." He jerked his shoulders free and moved closer to the painting.

"You cannot take the law into you own hands," Larry warned.

"Should I just sit around and wait for Emmett to kill me?" Hood shot back bitterly. "Is that Judge going to stand between me and Emmett's bullet? I think not!" Hood began to feel the comfort of the rage that had once defined him. His grandfather came to mind, and he slowly began to regain control of himself. He turned away from the painting and confronted Larry directly. "I know you mean well, and I thank you for your friendship, but I am alone. The law cannot protect me from Emmett. I will do what I have to do to survive."

Larry wasn't sure how to respond. He had been out-maneuvered in logic by a fifteen-year-old. He knew that Hood was right when he said that the law could not protect him. "I'll pray for you, Jedediah."

"I thank you, Larry," Hood said sincerely.

Larry handed Hood a bundle of clothes. "These are the clothes your dad was wearing the day he was shot. I thought you might want them. I bought a new suit for Jake to be buried in." His voice was somber. Hood accepted the bundle and nodded, wordlessly.

Hood started to leave and then he turned back. "Where is Pops buried?"

Larry smiled because he felt that Hood would be pleased. "On your land," he hesitated, "by that spot you call Pretty Place."

Hood grinned so wide that he could feel his face stretch. "Thank you so much." Tears rolled down both of Hood's cheeks. Larry felt the tears springing up in his eyes as well. They gave each other a short, awkward hug, and Hood went on his way.

≫—23—→
A WING AND A PRAYER

Our Father in heaven, hallowed be your name, your kingdom come, your will be done, on earth as it is in heaven. Give us today our daily bread. Forgive us our debts, as we forgive our debtors. And lead us not into temptation, but deliver us from the evil one.

Jesus of Nazareth

RAINBOW ROCK is a massive formation caused by an upward fold of the rock strata. As the Jackson River undercut this particular mountain base over eons, large sections of rock fell away and dropped into the river. The exposed layers of cliff are undeniably shaped like a rainbow. Before the invasion of settlers, the Bald and Golden eagles considered this terrain to be prime nesting ground. The Cherokee tribes considered it to be a mystical place, and legend had it that a boy's passage into manhood often happened in this spot.

For better or for worse, time changes everything. Clifton Forge grew on one side of the great rock and Iron Gate on the other. The C&O Railroad put tracks alongside the Jackson River at the base of the cliffs. The eagles left for less inhabited areas and the Cherokee were pushed out as well.

Larry's office was only a half of a mile from Rainbow Rock, so Hood felt compelled to pay this spot a visit before he left town. He had so much to think about. Stimuli, some of it fantastic and some of it horrible, overloaded his mind. He had friends again—people who cared for him. The world didn't seem so empty and lonely, and yet, for him, the world was still a very dangerous place.

The letter from his dad, his Pops's own words, seared his heart with loss. The pain really never left completely, but now it was like a weight in his chest. He was so proud to be his dad's son. He was proud to be Cherokee as well. Why did his Cherokee blood bother so many people? Was he really that different? Hateful people like Emmett knew nothing of the Cherokee, nor did they want to learn. They had no desire to understand. They just wanted to steal the land from under their feet.

Hood felt a need to consult his father and forefathers. He needed wisdom and guidance. He felt true loathing in his heart. Although his grandfather, Larry, and now even his father—from beyond the grave—had tried to persuade him otherwise, it was revenge that he desired.

The feeling was a poisonous lust in his soul. What had been done to his Pops and his family was wrong, and justice wasn't going to be served by the powers that be. Sheriff Green had a just heart, but he was part of a system that couldn't allow him to do what he considered to be right. He was bound by the law.

Hood felt rage welling up within him. The anger twisted and turned through his stomach and rose up into his chest. He knew with a clarity he'd never felt before that he wanted to take the life of another man. He had been taught by the Lord and Savior that this was wrong, and he felt guilty that he couldn't let this vengefulness go. Oh, how he wanted to sin. He wanted to wield justice with his own hands. He wanted to stare into the dying eyes of Emmett Stone.

Hood sat on a boulder at the base of the cliff overlooking the river. He crossed his legs into the classic position. The water shimmered, but he stared past it, not really focusing on anything.

His Pops had implored him not to blame God. He saw no problem there. He wasn't angry with God or mad at the world. His hate was for Emmett and all those who took pleasure in the suffering of others. He felt a pang of hypocrisy, thinking of all the animals he had to kill for his own survival. All these mixed emotions and thoughts were overwhelming. He had no problem forgiving the Lord. That was never where he had cast the blame. Would God be able to forgive him? That was what he wondered. "Vengeance is mine, sayeth the Lord," he had read in the Bible. It was time to pray.

"Oh Great Spirit, Creator and Savior. I come to you with a troubled heart. So much evil and wrong has been thrust upon my family. Revenge is yours, I have been taught, but I want it for my own. I make no pact with the evil one as I make plans to do an evil deed. Please forgive this weakness within me. I shall always seek your grace. I beg of you to protect my mother and sister. They need your love and guidance. Be also with this little town that accepts me as I am. Please do not let my actions bring harm to any of them. I am a sinner begging for your forgiveness."

Hood finished his prayer, but his mind remained in a trance-like state. The air felt fresh and crisp in his nostrils. His ears were keen and sensitive to all the surrounding sounds. His eyes were closed, but he could see with his mind. He heard an eagle cry from a distant height, but wasn't sure if it was real or imagined. He could feel his negative emotions streaming away as he opened his eyes just in time to see an eagle's tail feather spin softly into his lap.

Hood sat for a while, holding the base of the feather with its tip to his chin. The breeze was a comfort as it rippled through his long, black hair and over his face and hands. His heart was lighter now than when he'd come, as though the wind had swept right through him, carrying his hate away and leaving behind a sense of peace. Reluctantly, he stood, and as he did, a train whistle sounded in the distance. He gazed down the hillside to see the train moving steadily in the direction of his home. As he started downhill, Hood smiled to himself, "Timing is everything."

24
REUNION

RUBEN FUDD was jumping out of his skin in the church pew. Preacher Tuck was delivering a follow-up sermon, reflecting on the funeral the day before. The good preacher was trying to promote a sense of healing in his injured little community. Fudd knew that Hood would be waiting at the snake-bite spot and he wanted to be on his way. Two days in a row at church felt a bit excessive.

Finally, church was dismissed. He picked up his rifle from his dad's horse and buggy and gave his mom a quick kiss on the cheek. His father, Bill Fudd, gave him some parting words. The gist of the message was to be home an hour after dark so he wouldn't worry Mother Fudd.

"Yes, sir," Fudd said as he turned to leave. "Come on, Buddy."

Buddy let out one excited bark and hopped out of the buggy seat. He had been waiting patiently throughout the church service.

It was eleven o'clock when church let out, and Fudd knew he could easily cover the three miles in one hour and meet up with Hood. Buddy always seemed to know where they were going, and he took off in the lead.

Hood was cooking up some fish when Fudd and Buddy walked into the small campsite. The cast iron pot of coffee was sitting in the coals of the fire. Fudd noticed that Hood was still wearing his denim pants, but now he also wore his moccasins and buckskin vest. Buddy ran up to Hood joyfully, and Hood rubbed him behind the right ear just like he liked it.

"Looks like you spent the night here," said Fudd as the two boys greeted each other by extending their right hands and locking forearms.

"The fish are just about ready," said Hood as he worked around the cooking fire. The fish were splayed on sticks and the skin was starting to look crisp.

Fudd inhaled deeply. "Coffee smells good," said Fudd, "What can I do to help?"

"The dishes when we're done," said Hood, and both boys laughed.

After Fudd finished the dishes, they decided to scout around a little to see if there was any sign of the mountain lion. Fudd said that he had seen three sets of hunters in the woods on his way over. "I reckon they're looking for the cat."

Hood thought the best place to look for signs would be up higher in the mountains. He believed the mountain lion only came down low if she was really hungry or if it was dry and she needed water.

"It hasn't rained since the night you got me to the doctor," Fudd noted.

"I'm surprised you even knew it rained," Hood replied. "You were halfway to the Pearly Gates by the time the rain started."

"I faded back into consciousness every now and again. It was a bit of a bumpy ride if I remember rightly. Most of all, I remember that you saved my skin that night."

If the cat were in search of water, the boys knew it could be anywhere, so they decided to keep a sharp eye below them as they worked their way up into the mountains. Fudd picked up his Hawkins gun and Hood reached for his bow and quiver of arrows.

"You take the long shots," said Hood, "and I'll handle the up close and personal." Hood patted the knife on his side and both boys smiled slyly. They were going to make a good team. As they started up the path, Buddy jumped into the lead. He was a team member, too.

⟫—25—→
THE EYE OF THE LION

THE MOUNTAIN lion watched as the horse and rider slowly made their way down the mountain trail. The rider's head was looking down, studying the terrain. He would not be hard to get the jump on. The sun felt warm on her fur as she stretched out on the rock shelf overlooking the path. The rider was coming right to her. She closed her eyes and turned her face into the afternoon sun. She flicked her tail lazily. She preferred her prey to be a bit smaller, but she felt little fear of any creature. Stealth was her way of life. She didn't like to be seen until it was too late. She stretched out her lean and lanky body and slowly eased to her feet. Then she left the area. The rider never even knew she was there.

★ ★ ★

The boys had been scouting and climbing for about two hours when Buddy froze in the middle of the trail ahead of them. Fudd grabbed Hood by the arm and nodded toward his dog. The fur on Buddy's neck was raised in hackles. He stood motionless and made no sound.

Fudd leaned in and whispered into Hood's ear. "Buddy says there's something up ahead."

Hood acknowledged him with a nod of his head, and they began scanning the woods around them in silence. Fudd had his rifle resting with the barrel in the crook of his left elbow and his right thumb ready to pull back the hammer. Hood had an arrow knocked up, but there was no need to pull back on the string until he saw something. No one moved for what seemed like an eternity because Buddy would not call off his alert.

Finally, the sound of a horse murmur broke the silence and a faint clip-clop could be heard as a rider slowly moved down the trail. The rider came into view, and Hood whispered to Fudd, "I know him." Both boys relaxed slightly. It wasn't Emmett.

The rider saw Buddy and halted in his tracks.

"T.R.!" Hood called out.

"That you, Hood?" responded the rider.

"Yes, sir, it is."

The fur on Buddy's back dropped and his demeanor relaxed. He ran back to Fudd to make sure everything was okay.

"I see you have some friends with you," T.R. observed as he drew his horse nearer to the small hunting team.

"This here is my friend, Ruben Fudd, and his dog, Buddy."

T.R. reached down from his horse and shook hands with Fudd.

"I heard about your snakebite incident," said T.R. "Looks like you came out on top."

"Yes, sir," said Fudd. "I'm doin' just fine."

Fudd took note as Buddy made his way up the trail once again and came to a halt with his nose into the wind.

Hood questioned T.R. about the trail ahead. "Did you see any signs of that mountain lion?"

"No sign at all, not even a track," T.R. said with disappointment. "She must be down low or…"

"Buddy thinks somethin' else is lurkin' about," Fudd interrupted.

Everyone's head turned toward Buddy and their communication was cut to a whisper.

T.R. dismounted his horse and led it by its reins. The group cautiously followed Buddy, and he led them to a track that was, undeniably, that of a mountain lion.

"I just came this way moments ago. That beast was probably watching me," said T.R.

"If the cat knows we are here, then we won't be able to close in on her on foot," said Hood.

T.R. let out a low, almost silent whistle. "She's staying a lot lower than I expected."

Fudd voiced what all three of them were thinking: "She's been getting a lot of food down here."

"Should we spread out and try to herd her past one another?" asked Hood.

"Good strategy." T.R. nodded his head in support of the idea.

Hood picked up a stick and drew the movements that each person would make. They would form a big triangle in the woods and every half hour one person would move at a time. With luck, the one moving would push the mountain lion past one of the other two. Without luck, they might get attacked. They all knew they were hunting an animal that could hunt them back.

Hood's first location covered a well-worn game path. The mountain lion might use it as an escape route if it saw one of the other hunters. He could also see into a meadow in the valley below. It wasn't his turn to lead the drive for about fifteen minutes. Then a movement in the valley below caught his eye.

Five horsemen were riding along at a pretty good clip. They came to the edge of the meadow and halted abruptly. Just then, a sixth horseman emerged from the tree line to face the other five.

Hood descended toward the group to see if he could get a better look. He crouched low and took off at a slow jog. As he got closer, he slowed down even further and proceeded with more caution.

He came within sixty yards of the riders but dared not get any closer. The trees were getting thinner toward the opening of the meadow and there wasn't much cover. He could hear the men speaking, but was having trouble making out the words. One of the riders turned toward him, and Hood could see his face for the first time. It was Emmett Stone. Hood's blood turned to ice. He could feel the hate surge within him. They were up to no good, and Hood could sense it.

Emmett turned his attention back to the lone rider who had come out of the woods. This man appeared to be the leader of the group. Hood leaned forward, straining to hear what was being said. He could only pick up snippets of the conversation. He distinctly heard the words "train number eight" and "meet at Eagle Rock." Hood tried to get a good look at the leader, but he was facing in the other direction. The group disbanded and the sixth horseman turned and rode toward Hood. The other riders went back toward Iron Gate, the direction that they had come from.

The leader was going to come uncomfortably close to Hood's hiding place. He felt a surge of adrenaline course through his body, and he flattened himself down as best he could. He was on his back with his bow half drawn and lying across his belly. The rider came within ten yards of Hood and brought his horse to a stop. Hood dared not move a muscle. He felt exposed, as he had not expected anyone to come this direction. The horseman looked beyond Hood, in the direction the other riders had taken. Hood could see his face clearly now. Then the horseman moved on. The face was not one he recognized.

A short while later, T.R., Fudd and Hood reconvened to discuss the hunt. T.R. said he hadn't seen a thing.

Fudd said, "Squirrels."

Hood said, "Well, I saw plenty, but it wasn't the mountain lion!" He recounted what he'd just witnessed.

"What do you think they're up to?" inquired Fudd.

"Could be anything or nothing," T.R. surmised with a shrug. "Best thing to do is just stay clear. They could be hunting for the mountain lion just like we are."

"I don't know," said Hood. "It just seemed suspicious. Something doesn't feel right."

"There really isn't much that we can do or should do," said T.R. "It's not illegal to meet in the woods and talk." Finally, the group let the subject drop and began the journey back toward Hood's property.

It was starting to get dark and Fudd said he'd best break away where they were and get started for home. As he and Buddy said their good-byes, he turned to Hood and said, "My mother wants to fix you a meal since you saved my life. I practice for the rodeo on Wednesday after school over at the Highland's ranch. You could meet me there if ya want and then we could go to my farm and git fed."

"Sounds like a plan!" said Hood with a smile. "Can't pass up a free meal."

"Oh it ain't free," chuckled Fudd. "You got to do the dishes when we're done."

★ ★ ★

T.R. and Hood decided to share a camp for the night. They continued on toward Hood's land. With Emmett and the Cowboys lurking about, they decided to get off the beaten path and keep their fire small.

"Mr. Hood," T.R remarked as he tended his horse for the evening, "I was glad to hear that you like to read." He reached into his saddlebag. "I have a book here about the adventures of Kit Carson. Would you like to hold onto it for me for a while?"

Hood lit up excitely. "We used to read about Kit Carson in school! We read all the news about the Western frontier in Miss Summers's class! We used to read books and newspapers all the time!"

T.R. handed Hood the book. *The Life and Adventures of Kit Carson* by DeWitt C. Peters, 1855.

Hood beamed from ear to ear as he flipped through the thick, cream-colored pages. Something about holding a book in his hands made him feel civilized. It had been four years since he'd so much as touched a book, but he knew he was an accomplished enough reader to work through this one.

As T.R. watched on, he noticed the smile on Hood's face melt away and his demeanor darken. Hood was staring past the book now, totally lost in thought. His whole civilized world had been taken from him. He was a surviving victim of his father's murder and yet, he had been labeled "savage." He was the outcast.

"Jedediah, you okay?" Hood turned his head toward T.R. and snapped back to the moment.

"Yeah, I'm fine." He looked down at the book in his hand. "Thank you for the book. I haven't read one in a while." He walked over to his bedroll and tucked himself into a cozy little burrow. The sky was clear and full of stars. Hood fell asleep quickly. He'd been out for several hours by the time the dream started. It was one he'd had many times before.

"Jedediah," his Pops said to him, "let's head over to the Trading Post." They said goodbye to Lawrence and walked out of his law office. Down the street they went. Jake and Jedediah. His Pops took the bowler hat off of his head and put it on his son's. It was too big and it covered his eyes. Hood adjusted it so that he could see.

Jake said, "I believe I'll buy me a new hat today at the Trading Post." They were both smiling. It was a beautiful day. As they neared their destination, the Trading Post sign swung gently in the breeze. He could feel the warm air on his face. They were almost to the Dew Drop Inn...

BANG! A shot rang out.

Hood looked around to see what was going on. Pops had stopped walking. He stood stock-still with a strange, far-away look on his face, and Hood felt a sudden pang of fear. Jake dropped to his knees, his arms hanging limply at his sides. A small spot of blood appeared and began to spread across the front of his shirt. Then he toppled over and rolled onto his back, his face to the sky.

Hood knelt on the ground beside his father. His eyes were wide open, gazing straight ahead, without a hint of recognition. Hood had seen that look many times before when he was hunting. It was the cold, vacant stare of death.

Hood awoke in a cold sweat. This was the part of the dream when he always woke up. Hood hated that he had to relive the terror of that day over and over again. He drew his knees up to his chest and buried his face in them.

He hardly enjoyed the hunt anymore because of the dream. Every time he saw the eyes of his kill, it reminded him of his father. Now, hunting was something he did merely to survive, and when he was done, he felt despair for his prey. The only eyes he wanted to see with that look belonged to Emmett Stone. He raised his head to see T.R. looking down at him.

"Bad dream?" inquired T.R.

Hood nodded, "Yeah."

Nothing more was said. Hood lay staring at the sky for a while before he finally drifted back to sleep.

When T.R. woke up the next morning, Hood was reading.

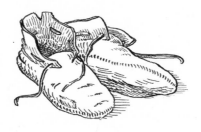

⟫—26—→
OCTOBER MORNING

THE NEXT few days went by quickly. Hood and Oliver worked tirelessly rebuilding the barn and gathering firewood. They would have to collect a lot more wood to prepare for a long, cold winter. Hood was beginning to live openly in the barn. He'd seen no sign of Emmett or his gang since he'd last spied on them in the meadow, and it felt good not to be living in hiding. It had been several days since Hood had seen anyone, come to think of it. T.R. spent most of his time in the high country looking for the mountain lion, and Hood's other friends were busy with school and harvest time.

This morning Hood was up before the crack of dawn. His food supply was getting low, so he was preparing for a hunt. Morning had always been his favorite part of the day. He loved to watch the earth wake up and come to life. The sun's rays had not yet penetrated the horizon. Stars and a three-quarter moon still hung suspended in the sky. Hood carried his bow today instead of his rifle. If Emmett and the Cowboys were nearby, his bow would not betray his location the way a rifle would. He was dressed as a Cherokee. He felt more in tune with the forest with moccasins on his feet. He still wore his bowler hat, but had noticed recently that it was starting to show serious signs of wear. The lining was threadbare and tearing, and the brim sagged where once it had been tight and trim.

Hood had a good idea of where he wanted to go. It was probably his favorite spot in the whole world, and it meant even more to him now that he knew Pops was buried nearby. He moved quickly. He wanted to be in position before it was light enough to see. Within minutes, Hood stood on a plateau overlooking a ravine. A great pine tree towered before him. This was a good place to hunt since deer liked to use the ravine for traveling to and from the river. Hood had killed his first deer here at age seven, but that wasn't the reason he loved this place.

His Pops had brought him to this spot for the first time when he was five. That very first, bone-chilling morning, they got there before dawn. He could hardly contain his excitement. His Pops thought he was old enough to hunt. He couldn't believe it. Pops had to continually shush him so he wouldn't scare everything away. Together, they cleared the needles and debris away from the base of the great pine, creating a full circle so they could move around the tree without making noise.

His Pops kept telling him to listen to the forest, and he tried. They sat in pitch-black darkness. The stillness of the forest was absolute. "I can't hear nothin', Pops," he had whispered into his father's ear.

"That's right. But keep listening. The forest will wake up soon," his Pops had said.

Then the sun's rays started to peek over the horizon. At first all Hood could make out were shadows, but those shadows slowly developed into trees. A great horned owl hooted from a nearby perch.

"It knew we were here the whole time," Pops whispered into his ear.

Fat little chickadees started bouncing from branch to branch. They fussed and darted and dove here and there. Squirrels started chattering next. They chased each other, swirling around the trunks of trees. One squirrel came down the trunk of their tree and almost jumped on their heads before it realized they were there. Bark chips had gone down the collar of his shirt when the squirrel slammed on the brakes.

As the sun's brilliance fully lit the area, it was the most beautiful setting that Hood had ever seen. The ravine was lined with mountain laurel. Small pine, hemlock and cedar trees were scattered along the mountain face that rose beside them, a light dusting of snow bringing contrast as it settled into the evergreen branches. "This is a pretty place, Pops," he had said, awestruck by the beauty of his surroundings.

"Why don't we call it that then?" Pops had suggested.

"What?"

"Pretty Place."

So they had named that spot Pretty Place. Other spots got named in a similar fashion. Turkey Ridge was so named because they had seen a large flock of turkeys there one morning. Bear Creek was so named because they watched a mother bear and two cubs drink and play in the water.

Now, Hood could almost feel his Pops's presence as he scraped the leaves away from the base of the tree. He glanced around, wondering where he would find the grave, but it was still too dark to tell. He heard an owl off in the distance and wondered if it was the same owl. A whippoorwill called into the darkness. The sun's rays peeked through the horizon. Two Bobwhite Quail scurried nearby. The chickadees started chirping and bouncing from branch to branch.

Hood sat down, resting his back against the tree's rough trunk. Now that he finally had time to sit still, thoughts flooded his mind. Sure, bad things had been happening, and his anger toward Emmett still burned in his chest, but there were plenty of other things to dwell on too. Hood scanned the horizon, watching for movement. He blew into the cups of his hands as his mind wandered to all the good things the past week had brought: Katy's pretty smile, Fudd's friendship, the book from T.R., and most of all, the letter Pops had left behind. He loved the feeling of the sun as its first rays warmed his face. Then his eyes fixed on a small, discrete headstone almost close enough to touch. No wonder he felt such a strong presence of his father. A tear rolled down his cheek and entered the upturned crease of his smile. He would be able to hunt this spot with Pops for the rest of eternity.

An hour of daylight had passed before he noticed a slight movement in the distance. A doe and two fawns ambled along slowly in his direction. The fawns still had spots. One fawn kept pestering his mother for some milk and she finally relented. They still needed their mother. Hood let them pass. He enjoyed spying on this beautiful moment in nature. They had come within twenty yards of him and never realized he was there. Hood kept a keen watch to see if father buck was shadowing the group. It wasn't long before he picked up more movement in the underbrush.

Two coyotes were following the same path as the deer. They moved with purpose, their noses to the ground. Hood knocked up an arrow, but he couldn't get a clear shot. They slipped by him and the opportunity was lost. He knew the fawns would have little chance. Almost instinctively, an idea jumped into his brain. Hood drew the string of his bow back and made his best imitation of a fawn bleat. The ears of both coyotes perked to attention, and they turned and charged in Hood's direction. Hood let his arrow fly and watched as the arrow pierced the lead animal. The coyote howled in pain and started spinning in circles, trying to pull the arrow out with its teeth. The second coyote could see that the first was injured and did not hesitate to attack his former ally. His friend was now food. Hood knocked up a second arrow but the uninjured coyote caught his movement and dashed away in an instant. Hood walked over and finished off the first.

It was unfortunate to have to kill an animal that he did not intend to eat, but the coyote was a threat to his very existence. Not because it could kill him—that was unlikely—but because they would kill or run off his food supply. They would kill livestock as well, if given the opportunity. The coyotes would have to balance out the food chain somewhere else. As he skinned the pelt so it wouldn't go to waste, he reflected on the fawns and the legend his grandfather had told him long ago. He was glad that the fawns would live to see another day.

Hood decided that Pretty Place was played out for the day. He had another location he wanted to try. He stood by his father's grave and said with an uplifted spirit, "I will be back to visit with you soon." Then he turned his face to the sky and recalled the words he'd often used to comfort himself since his father's death: "He is always with me." With that thought, he moved along.

Shirkey Mill Branch is fed by a large watershed, and Hood had never seen it run dry. As he approached the creek, he removed his moccasins. The water was swift and cold. He took great pleasure in standing in the creek he had so often played in as a child. He examined the water more closely and saw a school of minnows dart behind a large rock that breached the water's surface. A crawdad raised his pincers as the minnows went by, but it was a feeble attempt to catch one. This would be a good spot to procure some bait for his next fishing foray.

Hood climbed Turkey Ridge by following a deer trail. Deer pellets sat in piles everywhere. He noticed some small cedar trees that had been horned by a buck. Acorns littered the ground, providing the deer an excellent food supply. This was an active area and an excellent spot to take a stand. He had just gotten comfortable when he heard a twig snap in the distance. His heart quickened as light steps in the leaves moved closer and closer. Hood saw a figure moving cautiously through the low-lying scrub brush. Hood's arrow flew true and he got his buck.

»—27—→

THE HIGHLAND RANCH

AS HOOD dragged the buck back to his farm, he reflected that this would be the first skin he could trade at the Trading Post. It gave him a feeling of independence. He was supposed to meet Fudd at the Highland's ranch soon, so he would have to put off the skinning 'til the morning.

He didn't want to admit it to himself, but he was nervous about going to the Highland's ranch. He had been there plenty as a young boy, but now his motive for being there was a little more complicated. The arrangement was to meet up with Fudd, but Katy would be there and it plagued his mind and his stomach with turmoil.

He cleaned himself up in the creek, once again thinking it odd that a girl could have him bathin' all the time. Then he put on his jeans and his Pops's blue shirt.

On his way out of the barn, he started to reach for his bow and hesitated. He wasn't sure why, but he didn't want to look like a Cherokee to Katy or her family. He felt like a hypocrite and a sell out, but he still put the bow back in its place and reached for the Winchester instead.

He asked Oliver, "Do I look like a fool of phenomenal proportions?"

Oliver nipped Hood's leg in response.

"Thanks," Hood muttered. He lightly smacked the animal's behind and started off for the Highland Ranch.

★ ★ ★

Fudd was racing Jett Highland around the barrel course when Hood arrived. He barely beat her, even though she was half his age. Jeanette Highland, or Jett, as she was most often called, was already an accomplished rider.

Hood leaned his rifle against the fence and climbed to the top rail. He took a seat and watched. Jett challenged Fudd to another race, and he accepted. They trotted back toward the starting line.

Hood surveyed the ranch from his perch on the rail. The fields were full of corn that looked ready to harvest. The garden was positioned closer to the house and was bustling with activity. Mrs. Veronica Highland was instructing a couple of farmhands on how to pick the cabbage. In a field just beyond them, Ellie and Katy tended a pumpkin patch. Just seeing Katy, even from such a distance, made Hood's heartbeat quicken.

Clete Highland walked out of the barn with his twelve-year-old son, Chip. Chip was leading a horse that had just been saddled. It was Lightning. Clete noticed Hood sitting on the rail and gave him a nod. Hood tipped his bowler hat in return. Clete told Chip to take the horse to the water trough and then walked over to greet Hood. Hood hopped down from the rail, wondering why he felt so nervous. He had known Mr. Highland most of his life.

"I see that you grew up while you been gone, Jedediah." Clete extended his hand and Hood shook it.

"I see that you still got more work to do than a mere mortal can handle," Hood said in response. Hood no longer felt the tension that had been building within him.

"Funny you should mention that," Clete said with a grin. "I just lost a couple of ranch hands."

Chip rode up on the outside of the coral and stated, "I'm glad that

Zeb and Lester are gone, even if it is harvest time." Then he looked at Hood. "Howdy, Jedediah. Good to see ya again."

Hood returned the greeting.

"Daddy taught them boys how to bronco ride and they ran off to join the rodeo." Chip puffed up his chest. "I'll be old enough to bust bronco next season."

"That's great," Hood said to Chip. "Then you can teach me how to bust."

Chip beamed with pleasure at the prospect of being a trainer like his dad.

Hood turned to Clete, "Well, maybe you better quit teaching your work crew how to ride and rodeo and they might have more interest in the fields. Rodeo is a mite more fun."

"No doubt, those boys thought so too," Clete laughed. "But I'm not a believer in all work and no play."

"GO!" yelled Jett, and the race was on. Both riders dashed for the first barrel. Fudd got there first, but Jett took the corner better and came out of the turn with a slight lead. Fudd's hat flew off as the horses picked up speed. Jett carried a good line into the second barrel and built a two-horse-length lead as they flew toward the third barrel. Fudd knew he was beat unless she made a mistake, so he kept the pressure on. Jett overshot the third barrel by just a smidge, but it was the opportunity that Fudd had hoped for, and he was in position to undercut her in the turn. He spurred his horse lightly as they came out of the turn and he coasted across the finish line first.

"Dag Nabbit!" yelled Jett as she crossed the line a split second too late. She was feuding mad that she'd been beaten again. Fudd reveled in his victory, smiling broadly as he trotted over to Hood and Mr. Highland.

"That little Jitterbug beat me twice last week!" Fudd exclaimed to Hood. "Better her mad than me." He gave Mr. Highland a knowing wink.

Mr. Highland laughed as he appraised his youngest daughter. "Give her another year and she will beat you every time, Ruben."

"Oh, I don't think she's willin' to wait a year." Fudd believed that it was true. Jett would one day rule all the riding events at the rodeo.

Jett trotted over to the rail and brought her horse alongside Fudd. She looked across the rail at her father and then at Hood. "Hey, Jedediah," was all she said to him, as though she'd seen him just last week.

"I challenge you to another race, you big goon," she said, turning her attention back to Fudd.

Fudd said nothing. He just smiled and turned his horse toward the starting line. Fudd kicked his left leg over the neck of his horse and slid down the horse's right side. He picked up his hat off the ground and beat it on his riding chaps. Dust flew everywhere, then he slowly and deliberately placed it back on his head. Jett was getting impatient at the starting line, so Fudd took his time and made her wait. He shot a mischievous glance over to Clete and Hood and then remounted.

Hood felt a hand lightly touch his back and he turned to see Mrs. Highland standing behind him. Hood quickly removed his hat. Veronica gave him a warm hug and then stood back to look at him.

"Would you look at how tall he has grown, Clete? My goodness he looks like he could lift a horse."

"I don't know about liftin' horses, but he does look strong enough to pick some corn," Clete hinted again that he needed help with the harvest.

"Clete, you leave that boy be about the corn. He hasn't been here in four years. He came here to visit, not to work."

Hood shifted on his heels, uncomfortable under all the attention. To add to his nervousness, the twins were approaching.

"Would you look at what the cat drug in?" Ellie said with delight as she wiped the sweat from her brow.

"More like what the mountain lion drug in if you were to ask me," said Katy. She had a sassy look on her face, but her eyes were smiling. Hood's heart quickened once again.

Clete glanced back and forth at his daughters' smiling faces and realized that his twin girls were seeing young men in a brand new light.

His eyes rolled as he looked at his wife. "Good Lord, protect me from boy-crazy girls."

"Go!" yelled Jett as she and Ruben started another race. Eight hooves pounded the dry earth and dust billowed up around the spectators.

"DAG NABBIT!"

"ROYAL!"

»—28—→
MEET THE FUDDS

MOTHER FUDD loved to cook. "Three square meals a day keeps working men working," she would often say. Ruben would joke that she was the General of the house and his father was the General in the fields...that is, unless Mother Fudd was there.

The dessert for tonight's meal was her famous deep-dish apple cobbler. She had just removed the Dutch oven from the fire and the smell permeated the house. A large beef tenderloin was ready for the spit as soon as the boys showed up from rodeo practice. The freshly picked potatoes and corn would complete a hearty meal for two growing boys and her husband. She felt a touch of sadness at the thought that of her four boys, three had already left the nest. Ruben would be on his own before long as well, she suspected. She would soon be cooking small meals for just her and her husband, Billy.

The sound of Buddy barking alerted her that Ruben and his new friend had arrived. She removed her apron, straightened her housedress and brushed the hair from her face with the back of her hand. Then she opened the door.

Billy heard Buddy's barks as well. He exited the barn to greet the boys. Buddy ran up to him and he patted the dog's head before turning his attention to the boys.

"This is my dad," Fudd said as they converged in front of the barn.

"You can call me Billy. We're a might informal around the homestead."

"Thank you kindly, sir," Hood responded. "Please call me Jedediah."

Billy's hands enveloped Hood's in a vigorous shake. Billy led the boys toward the house where Mother Fudd waited in the open doorway.

"I'm just delighted that you could pay us a visit," Mother Fudd began. Hood took off his hat as they walked up the steps to greet her. "You are a hero to this family for saving my Ruben."

"Maw, you promised you wouldn't make a fuss about that if he came to supper," Ruben protested, rolling his eyes.

"Well, I had to thank him for savin' my baby boy, didn't I?" She knew that she was embarrassing him but she found it amusing. "Fact is, he is a hero." She walked up and hugged a slightly startled Hood. He had to slide his hat quickly out of the way to keep it from getting crushed.

"Better be easy with the hero stuff, Maw. We don't want his head to get too big for his hat." Fudd was enjoying seeing that Hood was just as uncomfortable as he was.

As Mother Fudd released Hood from her embrace, she took an appraising look at him and smiled. "My Christian name is Jessica, but everyone in this town calls me Mother Fudd, even Pastor Tuck." She shook her head and said, "I'm not sure why."

"'Cause you are a mother hen to everyone who lives in this town, Jessy," said Billy. She shot him a silencing look, and the three guys exchanged conspiratorial glances, trying not to smile.

"Into the house with the lot of ya!" Mother Fudd quickly reasserted control of the situation.

The dinner was delicious. Hood had not eaten beef since he had fled to live with the tribe. The Fudds told him about events he had missed in his absence, and Hood recounted some of his happier stories of living with the tribe. The warmth of the room was a great comfort. It felt

126

wonderful to sit at a family dinner table and have casual conversation. Mother Fudd bustled about attending to every detail. Hood could see how she had gotten her nickname; she did like to dote on those around her. Hood volunteered to do the dishes, but she would have nothing of it.

Hood was offered a bed for the night but he politely declined. "I have to take care of Oliver, my mule." He thanked them all for their hospitality.

"Will we see you at church on Sunday morning, Jedediah?" Mother Fudd inquired with a look that reminded him of his own mother's demand that he attend Sunday service.

"I reckon so," said Hood, as he saw no easy way of avoiding the issue.

"Royal," said Fudd. He enjoyed watching Hood squirm under the authority of Mother Fudd.

→ 29 →
ENTER THE CHAMELEON

IT WAS Sunday morning, and Hood was preparing himself for his invitation to church. He was as nervous as a long-tailed cat in a room full of rocking chairs, but he wanted to see his friends. He was going to wear the clothes that his Pops had worn the day that he was shot, the clothes that Larry had given him when he was at his Law office. They fit him well. Hood had cleaned them immaculately and painstakingly repaired the bullet hole in the back of the coat, making it virtually unnoticeable. He would look like any other parishioner in the church.

Hood thought about his Cherokee spirit animal. His grandfather had often told him that he had the eyes and senses of an eagle and that one day he would soar like the eagle as well. He felt that his spirit animal was confirmed on the day at Rainbow Rock when the eagle feather landed in his lap—the day he became a man.

Strangely, Hood felt that he could also identify with the chameleon lizard. He had seen one once as a child. It was in a box as part of a travelling animal show. The showman would put the lizard on a board painted green and the lizard would slowly turn green right before his very eyes. Then he would put the lizard on a board painted brown and the lizard would slowly change to brown.

This is how Hood felt as he put on his father's clothes. The townsfolk would accept him more easily if he dressed as they dressed. His features were such that he could look white or Cherokee depending on how he dressed. This was not the case for his mother and sister. They looked Cherokee through and through. He felt like he was part of two different worlds. Part of both but not fully accepted by either. He was the chameleon, just trying to blend in.

Hood felt incredible apprehension as he walked through the front doors of the church. A trickle of sweat rolled down the back of his neck. He felt the weight of the congregation's eyes as everyone turned to see what was causing the commotion. The crowd murmur raised a couple of octaves. People cupped their hands and whispered in their neighbor's ears, as if this would hide what was being said.

After a moment's pause, he proceeded down the middle of the aisle with his bowler hat held respectfully in his hands in front of his belly, his long, wavy black hair clean and brushed. He stopped at the pew where he had sat regularly with his family. He entered and took his seat.

There was a sudden shuffle and commotion as Colonel Deacon Sanders stood angrily and forced his wife and five children to exit the church. It was obvious that he wanted to protest loudly, but the setting of the church seemed to bind his tongue. His face was red with rage and insults slipped from under his breath as he pushed his family up the aisle and out of the church.

Billy Fudd and Clete Highland, although on opposite sides of the room, simultaneously stood up. Their families followed suit. But instead of leaving, both men led their families down the aisle, entered the pew where Hood sat and joined him.

The excitement level of the crowd grew noticeably, as no one knew what to expect next. Civil War scars were still pretty deep in this community and many in the room felt like battle lines were being drawn.

Shank Henry and his family were the next to stand. On his way out of the church, Shank paused at Hood's pew. With as much disdain as he could muster, he announced, "My family will not worship with a half-breed Indian mutt." Two other families got up and left the church as well.

Preacher Tuck quickly opted to change the message for the day. He raised his arms high and wide and spoke loudly over the roar of the congregation. "My brothers, my brothers. Listen to my words. The Lord Jesus chose to bring his word to the gentiles as well as the Jews, and because he was generous, he died for our sins and all others who seek his salvation. Fear not that some may chose this day to leave our church. A truly glorious gift has been given to us. There are some that may never understand this gift. Those who do not want this gift cannot have it forced upon them. As the apostle Paul said, 'If the gift is not received then wipe the sand from your sandals and move on.' Paul understood that some people don't actually want the message. They seek the praise of men or want to feel justified for their bad behavior. 'I tell you the truth,' said the good Lord Jesus. At times it may be necessary to empty the pews in order to fill them."

★ ★ ★

After church, a lot of people wanted to speak with Hood. Many commended him on his courage, but he didn't feel very brave. He just felt tired from all the attention. Still, he stayed and talked with everyone. He knew it was important to earn their acceptance. He was relieved when he and Fudd were finally able to make their exit. Buddy, of course, joined them and led the way back to Hood's farm.

"The barn looks ready for a dance," joked Fudd as he admired Hood's handiwork.

Hood beamed with pleasure at the compliment. When they walked around back, a six-point buck hung from a beam used to hoist hay to the barn's loft. It waited to be skinned and the meat butchered.

"I'll be pickled. That's the deer I was huntin' when I got snake bit!" Fudd exclaimed.

"It got by me that day too. I thought you might like to help me turn him into jerky. We can have us some tenderloin breakfast meat while we work."

"Sounds tasty," Fudd said as they both reached for the knives on their belts.

⟫⟫—30—→
A KISS OR A MISS

MONDAY AFTER school, Fudd and Buddy walked Katy and Ellie home. Clete Highland noted the return of his daughters and then turned his attention back to his crops. It was harvest time, and there was much work to be done. Veronica Highland was working in the garden close to the house. She was mad because the deer had gotten through the fence again and eaten some of her tomatoes. If this kept up there wouldn't be anything left come canning time.

Veronica yelled to her girls to change out of their school clothes and help in the garden. Katy said good-bye to Ruben and left to change. Ellie asked if she could visit with Ruben for a spell and maybe walk down to the creek.

Veronica wiped the sweat off her brow and put her hands on her hips. "Don't you be long, Miss Ellie Highland. The crop will rot on the vine if you don't get your chores done."

"I won't be long, Momma," Ellie replied gleefully. "I just want to get my feet wet and then I'll be ready to work.

Veronica was skeptical about her daughter's true intentions by the creek. Thank the good Lord that Ruben was a fine young man. "Ten minutes," was Veronica's final command.

"Yes ma'am!" Ellie and Fudd said at once, and off they went.

Ellie's blood rushed with excitement as they approached the creek. They were finally alone. Fudd sat down and untied his boots, and Ellie kicked her shoes off where she stood. When Ruben leaned his rifle against a tree and asked if he could hold her hand, she just about melted. The moment seemed magical. Hand in hand, they waded into the creek. The water was cold but added to the thrill of the moment. Ruben tugged gently on Ellie's hand so that she came about to face him, and then he grabbed her other hand as well.

Something about that freckly face and that goofy smile had always appealed to Ellie. It somehow conveyed an underlying confidence. He was a young man of simple, honest principle. She felt that he would always own her heart. She searched his face and noticed the red fuzz where his whiskers were starting to come in. She looked back into his eyes.

As Fudd returned her gaze, he noted with humor that his feet were cold and his palms were sweatin'. Then, with a fumbling tongue, he asked, "Miss Ellie, I sure would like to steal a kiss."

Ellie's knees felt weak as she stared into Ruben's eyes.

"It won't be stealin' if I give it to you."

As he leaned toward Ellie, Fudd thought to himself, or maybe it snuck out under his breath, "Royal."

Suddenly, a primordial yowl ripped through the air just above them. Fudd froze, inches from Ellie's lips, and stared past her in horror. His first thought was, "I don't have my gun."

He yanked Ellie behind him. The mountain lion was so close that they could see her muscles ripple under her gleaming fur as she slunk down from the rock where she'd lain in hiding. She began pacing the edge of the creek slowly, her long, thick tail whipping back and forth behind her. Her ears laid back and she bared her teeth as she let loose another blood-curdling scream.

Fudd's second thought was, "This is going to hurt."

All of a sudden, Buddy came out of nowhere like a big black ghost and slammed into the side of the cat, tearing at her neck with his teeth. The cat shoved him with her left paw and returned the favor with a swipe across the base of his neck and shoulder with her right. Buddy let out an audible yelp but pivoted and reengaged the attack by grabbing her right hind quarter in his jaws and ripping furiously. The mountain lion let loose another bone-chilling yowl. Fudd and Ellie could scarcely breathe. At this close range, the terrifying sound seemed to pierce right through them.

The two animals tore loose from one another and stood in a face-off at the water's edge. The cat's hindquarters were disheveled and splattered with crimson, and the hackles on Buddy's neck were matted with blood. Their chests heaved as they considered reengaging. Fudd and Ellie dared not move an inch. The only sounds now were the gurgling of the creek and the pounding of their hearts.

The cat was the first to break the standstill. She swung her massive head, gave the trio one last defiant look, and made off into the cover of the woods.

Ellie hugged Ruben Fudd tightly from behind as they watched the mountain lion slink off and disappear. Buddy walked into the creek and stood by his master. Both Ruben and Ellie leaned over and rubbed Buddy and checked out his wounds.

Clete Highland came running down the path with his rifle, grabbing Fudd's Hawkins rifle as he ran by it. There was a look of panic in his eyes. When he saw both kids and Buddy standing in the middle of the creek, his look changed to relief and then to resolve. He tossed Fudd his rifle and said, "I reckon that was the mountain lion I heard."

Ellie ran to her father and flung her arms around his waist.

"Daddy, it was only ten feet away. Ruben and Buddy saved me."

Clete glanced at the slashed-up earth and fur-strewn rocks on the opposite edge of the creek. He hugged his daughter tightly with his right arm and scanned the area.

"Buddy did all the work, sir," said Fudd. "I think I better have Doc

Larick take a look at him."

Fudd knelt down next to Buddy in the middle of the creek. Ellie walked back into the creek and her father followed. He didn't bother removing his boots. Ruben handed his rifle back over to Mr. Highland. As Fudd washed out Buddy's wounds he repeated over and over, "Thank you, Buddy. You're going to be all right."

⟫—31—→
THE GREAT TRAIN ROBBERY

EMMETT'S GANG of Cowboys watched with hungry eyes as the number eight train slowed to a halt. The huge oak tree lying across the tracks left Driver 8 with no other options. The tree was large enough to derail the train.

Once the train came to a complete stop, Driver 8 grabbed his bow saw and hopped down out of the engine. The train was heading to West Virginia, so all the coal cars were empty. It was his responsibility to deliver the payroll to the miners and then load up with coal and head east to all the towns along the tracks.

As Driver 8 approached the tree, he was concerned that this unexpected project would put him behind schedule. He would have to cut the tree into sections before he would be able to push his way through with the cattle guard. Then he noticed that the tree had been cut, and the root ball was not attached as it should have been if the tree had fallen of its own accord. His heart skipped a beat as he realized that this was a trap.

He never heard the shot; he just felt a small prick in his right upper chest. As he hit the ground, he thought about the day he met his wife.

Colonel Sanders heard the shot and bolted out of the caboose like a big white rocket. One of the Cowboys made a move to give chase, but Emmett called him off.

"Don't worry about that chicken, Lazarus. He hasn't seen who we are," Emmett said, even though he didn't particularly care if people knew whether it was him who robbed the train or not. This money was going to be his stake for going out West. A man with money and savvy could get lost out West. He could change his name and buy a cattle ranch. Even the boss wouldn't be able to track him down. He was, however, hoping to see that half-breed one more time before he made his exit.

The two men guarding the payroll watched as the Cowboys approached the train. There were no other passengers on board. As the Cowboys worked their way through the cars towards them, the guards leveled their guns at the door, aiming to take down at least one or two of the robbers. It was the most they could hope for; their hand had been dealt, and they weren't getting off that train alive.

News of the train robbery quickly spread through Iron Gate, Glen Wilton and beyond. Colonel Deacon Sanders had described his own heroic actions and his flight from harm under sniper fire. He sat in the Dew Drop Inn and repeated his daring exploits to anyone who would listen. His efforts to thwart the robbery got more grandiose with each whiskey.

Driver 8 was still alive when help arrived but he was in bad shape. It was up to Doc Larick and God now. Driver 8's only words were, "It was Emmett."

The good doctor of Iron Gate was having a busy day. He had just finished patching up Buddy when news arrived that the train had been robbed and the engineer was coming in with a bullet wound. Buddy's wounds had been superficial. The shoulder that had been clawed was shaved, lathered and bandaged. He was going to be fine. The two guards weren't as lucky. They would be going to the undertaker.

Fudd and Buddy returned home with the news of the train robbery and the mountain lion attack. Billy and Mother Fudd sat calmly as Ruben laid out the details of both dangerous encounters. Their sleepy little town had been anything but sleepy this past week or so.

"I have to go back to the Highlands and warn them to be on the lookout for the Cowboys. Then I'm heading to the old Hood place and warning Jedediah and T.R."

Billy nodded proudly at his son. The boy seemed to be becoming a man right before his eyes. Mother Fudd was anxious, but she knew there was no stopping him. He had to protect those that he cared for.

"I don't think you should take Buddy with you," she said as she knelt beside him and rubbed his chin. "He looks like he needs some rest. I'll give him a bone and lay him down by the wood stove." She busied herself to keep her mind off of her worries.

Fudd got a slice of the apple cobbler that Mother Fudd had just pulled out of the Dutch oven and he wolfed it down. It was more like a third of the pie than a slice. Mother Fudd just shook her head as she watched him eat. Then she laid some beef jerky on the table next to him.

"Put this in your pack in case you get hungry later."

"Yes, ma'am."

Twenty minutes later he was jogging up the path to the Highland ranch, rifle in hand. It felt weird to not see Buddy in front of him leading the way.

Ellie's first concern was for Buddy, and everyone was relieved to hear that he was resting comfortably. The news of the train robbery came as a shock.

"Keep on guard, Mr. Highland," said Fudd. "Everyone thinks it was Emmett and his Cowboys that did it."

Mr. Highland strapped on his pistol and pulled two extra rifles from the closet. Everyone in his family knew how to handle a gun.

Fudd turned to leave and Clete walked outside with him.

"Ruben, I want you to take Thunder and Lightning with you to go get Hood. I don't want you boys to be on foot. Get in and out of there as quick as you can. Warn Hood that Emmett may be looking for him.

I'm gonna ride into town and talk to Sheriff Green. The old Hood place might be a good place to start looking for the gang."

They walked over to the barn and Clete pulled down two saddles from the stall rail. Once both horses were saddled, Fudd tried to mount Thunder. On both attempts to get a foot in the stirrup, Thunder bucked slightly and pranced nervously about. Clete laughed a little and said, "He don't take to people right at first but he's a fine riding' horse once he trusts you."

Fudd looked over at Lightning who stood calmly chewing on some grass as Thunder danced about. "I think I'll let Hood ride the Thunder Cloud."

Clete laughed heartily and said, "Old Thunder is a lot of horse."

Fudd mounted up on Lightning and Clete ran a tether line from Thunder over to Lightning's saddle. Ellie walked out of the house and stood next to her father. Fudd smiled, tipped his hat at the two of them, and gave Lightning a little giddy-up kick. As he pulled away, he heard Ellie say over his shoulder, "You watch your back, Ruben Fudd."

Fudd pulled back gently on Lightning's reins and brought her around a quarter. He tipped his hat once again and gave Ellie a confident smile. "That's the plan, Miss Ellie. That is the plan." He spun Lightning back around and they trotted on down the trail. Ellie could only watch as her new beau rode out of sight. She felt cheated that he hadn't stolen that kiss.

≫ 32 →

THE KIDNAPPING

EMMETT HAD eyes and ears in the town of Iron Gate. He wanted to know what the Sheriff knew, and Shank Henry was his ticket. Old Shank would sell out his own mother for some whiskey money.

News of the robbery, the murder of the guards and Driver 8's uncertain survival were the talk of the town. The last word uttered by Driver 8 could get Emmet hung. Shank didn't have to work too hard for his money, which was just how he liked it. He and the Colonel had been drinking buddies for years, so all he had to do was drink and listen.

The Colonel relished being in the spotlight. He described his many attempts to pull Driver 8 out of the line of fire, driven back by the Cowboy's bullets bouncing all around him. He claimed that the guards were locked up in the money car, and they had yelled for him to go get help. He reluctantly left the siege, figuring that it was the only way he could save the others. Then he used his prowess in the woods to outmaneuver the outlaws.

Shank met up with Emmett at a prearranged spot and time. He gave his report, "The Sheriff knows it was you. I got some free advice for ya. Grab a hostage, a little girl, just until you get clear of the area."

Emmett laughed slyly and smiled a crocodile smile at the grizzled, ugly Shank Henry. "I always did like you, Shank. You are truly a spineless and mean-spirited old wretch. I probably won't miss you a bit."

Shank cackled at the insult as if it were a compliment.

Emmett reached into his saddlebag and pushed a hidden revolver to the side. He had considered just shooting Shank and being done with him, but after Shank delivered such valuable, nasty advice he decided to pay a double portion of the fifteen silver coins he had promised in exchange for information. "Good riddance, you scum of the earth," said Emmett as he mounted his horse. He tossed Shank the sack of coins.

Shank laughed and counted his money. He was going to get drunk tonight.

Emmett questioned himself as he rode away, wondering why he didn't just shoot the old bastard and put him out of his misery. He laughed at himself for paying a double portion. Thirty silver coins. Shank was his Judas. That was funny. Well, Shank couldn't cause him any additional trouble at this point, anyway. He would probably get drunk, run his mouth and get caught as an accessory. He might be the only one to get caught. Now *that* would be funny.

Emmett rode toward the old Hood place. He traveled off of the beaten path, across the side of Rich Patch Mountain above Glen Wilton. It was slow going across the steep ridges, but it gave him a vantage point in case there was a posse nearby. Shank's idea of taking a hostage was growing on him. A little girl would do just fine and wouldn't be as much trouble as an adult. There were lots of little girls in Glen Wilton. He started his descent.

As Emmett neared Glen Wilton, it was starting to get dark. He figured he had about an hour of light left. Little girls would be doing their evening chores. The Highlands and the Gordons both had little girls. Any of the Highland girls would do just fine; although, they were known to be little spitfires. One of them could end up being more trouble than she was worth, especially if the boys decided to have a little fun with her. Maybe that Gordon girl would be the best one to grab. She was younger and would be easier to control. Emmett decided to try there first.

Emmett sat patiently atop his horse, watching the house from the shadows at the edge of the woods. Between him and the house stood the chicken coop, a small, clapboard shack with a fence around it. Sure enough, after a short spell, Madeline came outside with a basket to collect her eggs. This was too easy. He grabbed two bandannas and a length of rope from his saddlebag and watched as Madeline walked into the coop.

Madeline was thinking of her sister as she went about her chores. They used to do all their chores together. They had been such a good team. She missed Patricia so much. She looked into the first nesting box and there were four eggs. Reaching inside, she wrapped her hand around the closest one. As she did so, a shadow fell across her outstretched arm. Her dad must have come out to help her. He had done that a few times since Patricia had died.

Emmett grabbed her by the hair at the base of her neck and stuffed a bandanna in her mouth. Madeline felt utterly helpless as her body was slammed against the dirt floor of the coop. The force of the blow popped the bandanna out of her mouth, but the wind had been knocked out of her as well, and she could only choke out a weak scream. Emmett quickly stuffed the wadded cloth back into her mouth and tied her hands behind her back with a coarse rope. He held her down with his right knee. When she struggled, he drove his knee in harder. He tied a second bandanna around her face so that she couldn't spit the first one out.

Madeline soon quit resisting. She was easily overpowered. She felt a bolt of pain as Emmet grabbed her by her hair and by the knot that bound her hands and slung her to her feet. It was then that she got her first look at her captor.

Emmett watched a look of terror flash across her face, and he felt a small tremor of delight. Her expression quickly changed to one of loathing. Emmett put his hands on her shoulders and shoved her to her knees. He leaned over and held his face inches from hers and smiled. His gold teeth flashed in the light and his breath stunk. "I can see that you got some spirit in you, so I'm going to warn you only once. Don't you make no trouble or no noise. Nod your head if you understand."

Madeline nodded.

"I just want to get clear of this town and you are my ace in the hole. You be good and I'll let you go. You make enough noise for someone to hear and I may as well shoot you. Do you understand?" Madeline gave one curt nod of her head and Emmett dragged her back to her feet and toward the door of the chicken coop.

Emmett peered out into the evening light, looking for any sign of movement. There was no one in sight. Emmett ushered her around the corner and into the woods. When they got to his horse, he took the rope from behind her back and retied her hands in front of her. Then he hoisted her up and slung her over the horse's shoulders, just in front of the saddle. He had already moved the saddle back and re-cinched it in preparation. He was quickly in the saddle behind her with the reins in his hands and his arms wrapped around her. With no other way to hold on, Madeline dug her heels into the sides of the horse and blinked back tears as they galloped off into the high country.

Emmett felt rather pleased with himself as they made their way back to the gang and the money. Now he had to figure out how to double cross the Cowboys. He was thinking that this girl and a worked-up posse might just create an excellent diversion, allowing him to slip away.

When Emmett showed up at the meeting spot, he was relieved to see that all the boys were there. Lazarus had done his job. Emmett hated to be separated from the money even for a moment. He was sure that he wasn't the only one thinking, "I want it all."

The Cowboys were nervous and when Emmett showed up with a hostage, it didn't help the situation. Emmett demanded the money back from Lazarus. He wanted to be the one holding the money. Protests started to arise.

"Why don't you pay me and Bubba now?" demanded Irving. "We

can just disappear."

Emmett walked Madeline over to the small campfire. He sat her down on the ground, untied her mouth and hands, looked her in the eyes and pointed at her with his index finger. "Keep your mouth shut and just sit there."

Madeline nodded.

Emmett had been expecting a play on the money. "We got to meet up with the Boss. He's the one who does all the payin'."

Bubba spit out some tobacco juice and said, "What about you, Shotgun? You want your money now?"

Shotgun Staubach was the loner in the group. He sat alone on a log cleaning one of his pistols. His other pistol lay loaded on a stump right in front of him. He had never ridden with the gang before and was only there because the Boss Man had insisted on his presence. No one really knew where he stood. He was lean and agile, and his clothes looked worn and dusty from the trail. The stubble on his gaunt face and his hollowed eyes gave him a haunting appearance that said, "Don't mess with me, I'm dangerous." Irving and Bubba wanted him to pick sides but he just looked the band of men over and went back to cleaning his gun.

He never did quite understand why people called him Shotgun. It wasn't as if he had invented the dang weapon. He thought his nickname was funny. He much preferred his 1874 Sharps .55 caliber Big Bore Buffalo rifle, "Old Reliable." He wasn't going to get lured into picking sides. His job was to make sure that Emmett didn't run off with the money. He figured that Emmett would play his hand soon enough, and he wanted to keep his cards close to his chest.

Lazarus broke the silence, "Emmett runs the job."

Irving and Bubba whined some more but to no avail.

"We meet up with the Boss tomorrow," said Emmett. "We can make the girl ride on the money horse so everyone knows where the cash is at all times. We also need to have someone trail behind to keep a lookout for the posse. We can take turns with that." He looked over his gang.

He could tell he had them back under control again.

Emmett walked over to check on the money. Beside the extra horse lay heavily laden saddlebags full of gold and silver coins. The Boss had provided these special saddlebags, which could be locked. The locks were intact and the leather was uncut. "Good." Outsmarting the Cowboys was one thing, but for this plan to work, he'd have to outsmart the Boss as well. The Boss was a dangerous man with a lot of power and resources. He would be the toughest to hide from. But it was a big country out there. The Boss would never find him if he kept a low profile.

He reached into his own personal saddlebag and pulled out three pieces of jerky. He tossed one to Madeline. She caught it and ate it without a word. Emmett could tell that she still had some fight left in her. Soon it wouldn't matter if she got away or if he gave her to the Cowboys. He just needed her one more day and then he would be off with the money.

When Madeline finished her jerky, Emmett walked her over to a large oak tree and sat her down with her back to the base. He tied her hands behind the tree in such a manner that she couldn't reach any of the knots. Emmett threw a blanket over her and said, "Don't thrash about or you'll tighten the knots on your wrists and knock off your cover."

Madeline knew he was right. She just nodded.

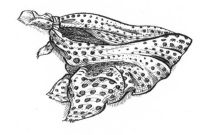

THE POSSE

THE FOLLOWING morning, the saloon at the Dew Drop Inn was packed to capacity. Many of the miners had ridden the train from West Virginia to Iron Gate to see what was being done to get their money back. Word was also out that Madeline Gordon was missing.

Shank Henry had gotten drunk at the Dew Drop Inn the night before and had talked himself into trouble. It seemed he knew a little too much about the girl's disappearance. He was now sleeping it off in the Iron Gate Jail. Emmett was the prime suspect in Madeline's disappearance, and Shank had pretty much confirmed it. His role in all this mess was yet to be determined.

Sheriff Green was doing his best to maintain control of the flaring tempers in the room. Many of the miners wanted to join the posse, but he would not allow it. He wanted a rescue party, not a lynch mob. He also explained that a smaller group would travel more quickly and track more efficiently. His posse was already handpicked, so he introduced them to the crowd.

Jon Rigger was a load of a man and well known as a top-notch logger, trapper and hunter. He received immediate approval from the crowd. Next, the Sheriff introduced T.R.. News of his prowess with a gun had spread through the area. He had already taken out one member of Emmett's gang when he shot Artimus Aikman. Everyone appreciated a fast gun. Xavier Duran stood up next. As the owner of the Trading Post, he was used to dealing with all types of characters, and he was respected as one who could handle the rough and tumble. Fletch Gordon was not to be denied a spot in the posse. Madeline was his daughter, and it was believed that the gang had taken her. He was known as a crack-shot who had fought bravely in General Lee's army. He was at Appomattox when the South surrendered. He had lost one daughter to the mountain lion and he was bound and determined to secure the safe return of Madeline.

When Ruben Fudd and Jedediah Hood walked into the circle from the back corner of the room, the attitude of the crowd shifted and became more confrontational. The miners looked at one another in disbelief. How could these kids hold their own against train robbers and killers?

"The boys were witnesses to a secret meeting of the gang in the woods. They are also familiar with Emmett's backhanded ways," said the Sheriff. Protests continued to arise. "They are more skilled in the woods than any of you mine dogs."

"Let the Half-Breed use those injin skills to get our money back," blurted out an oaf of a miner named Slick Miller. The rest of the miners in the room laughed.

Hood walked over to Slick and stood directly in front of him. He was wearing his Pops's good cowboy boots and denim jeans, a flannel shirt with the deer skin vest his mother had made over top, a red polka dot bandana around his neck and, of course, his bowler hat.

Slick stood about two inches taller than Hood, but when Hood got up in his face and said, "I'm half Irish and half Cherokee. What are you, some kind of blue-blood?"

Slick took a step back. Some of the miners laughed nervously.

Buddy moved toward the standoff and growled. The hair on his shoulders bristled up around his bandages.

Slick took another step back. He looked around the room for some kind of support, but there was none.

Fudd walked up to Buddy and rubbed the top of his head. "You want a piece of that, boy?"

Slick's eyes widened as he backed into the protection of the crowd.

"I think these boys can take on Emmett all right," observed Zackary Miller, Slick's brother. The miners in the crowd laughed once again, but a little uneasily.

"That is enough of that," the Sheriff intervened. Hood and Buddy and Fudd walked back and stood with the rest of the posse. This time, nobody objected. There seemed to be little doubt that this posse had the grit it would need to go up against the Cowboys.

As Fudd stood next to Hood, he whispered from the corner of his mouth, "Now that was royal." The corners of Hood's lips twitched into a smile.

Sheriff Green asked the posse to come down to the jail to be sworn in. The Fudd and Highland families looked on as the group of men took their oath. Both Hood and Fudd beamed with pride when the Sheriff pinned the deputy stars on their chests. The Sheriff had expressed reservations about Buddy coming with the posse but was soon convinced that the dog's tracking skills could be an asset. A low chuckle spread through the crowd when the Sheriff swore Buddy in and pinned a star to his bandaged shoulder. Buddy gave a howl of delight as he received his star.

The Sheriff approached Clete and Billy. "I'm concerned that the gang could double back, knowing that I have left town with a posse. I would feel much better if I knew that Iron Gate and Glenn Wilton had a protective watch."

Clete looked at his friend Billy, "Would you like to take charge of Iron Gate or Glen Wilton?"

"I'll take Iron Gate. You stick close to your family in Glen Wilton."

"Thank ya, Billy. That would make me a bit more comfortable."

Colonel Deacon Sanders had been eavesdropping on the Sheriff's conversation and thought that it should be he that laid out the defensive strategy for Iron Gate. He had already had a morning red eye or two at the Dew Drop, so he proclaimed with a slur, "I was born and bred to be a leader of men. I shall take control of Iron Gate."

Billy, Clete and the Sheriff looked incredulously at the Colonel. He stumbled slightly to his left.

"Why don't you guard the Dew Drop?" suggested the Sheriff.

"I shall take my post," the Colonel responded, and he spun on his heels and headed back toward the Dew Drop.

"I feel safer now that I know he's protecting the Dew Drop," said Billy with a sarcastic smirk.

"I feel even safer," added Clete, "knowing that he forgot his gun."

Sheriff Green tried to suppress a giggle, but it forced its way through his nose.

Larry Stewart approached the threesome, rifle in hand. "May I be of assistance, Sheriff?"

The Sheriff gave him a friendly pat on the shoulder and turned toward Clete and Billy. "Which one of you wants him?"

"I'll take him," Billy quickly responded, raising his hand.

The Sheriff nodded his approval as he made his way toward his horse. "Mount up, boys," he commanded, and he mounted his steed.

Mother Fudd was trying to hold back her tears as her son mounted up on Lightning. She was both proud and scared to death for her youngest son. She had to accept that he was now a man. She held her chin high and tried to appear strong.

Fudd could sense her turmoil and trotted over to where she stood. He dismounted and gave her the mighty embrace that she was longing for. He whispered a reassurance into her ear, "It will be all right mamma, I'll be really careful." He kissed her on the cheek.

She couldn't help herself and straightened the collar of his trail duster. He gave her a glowing smile and shook his head slightly from side to side, "I love ya, Mother Fudd. I'll be back before ya know it."

Fudd looked over to where his father stood, Winchester in hand with the barrel resting casually on his shoulder. He exuded strength and Fudd hoped to one day be just like him. Billy hadn't wanted to intrude on his wife's farewell. "Take care of yourself, son," he said as he approached. He extended his hand for a shake and Fudd batted it aside and hugged him unabashedly.

"Yes, sir, I'll do my best," he said as they came out of the embrace.

Fudd was about to mount Lightning when he was blindsided by Ellie Highland. She almost knocked him off his feet and his hat tumbled to the ground. She hugged him fiercely and kissed him on the ear. The expression on his face resembled shock, but his heart was soaring. She pulled back from his ear and looked directly into his eyes. She almost looked mad. "You better come back without a scratch or I'll kill you, Ruben Fudd."

"Yes, ma'am."

Suddenly, Ellie grabbed Fudd by the lapel of his duster and planted a kiss square on his lips. When she pulled away, Fudd had a wide-eyed, silly grin. "That awt to keep me thinkin' 'bout 'cha, Miss Ellie."

She seemed satisfied.

Clete watched on as Ellie said 'farewell' to Fudd. Then he turned his attention to Katy. She and Hood were strolling along hand in hand. He could not hear what was being said but he knew that she had deep feelings for this young man. Veronica wrapped her arms around him from behind and leaned her head against his shoulder. "Our girls are growing up, Clete."

He nodded and looked at his wife, "Do they both have to grow up the same day?"

"Well, they are twins."

He chuckled, "I reckon so."

Standing just a few yards away from Fudd and Ellie, Hood felt like the whole world was spinning. He was holding hands with Katy. If this moment were to last forever, then that was fine with him. It wasn't his imagination; she did have feelings for him. She pulled a neatly folded blue and white bandana from the pocket of her dress. "I know you already have one, but I wanted to give you a gift."

Hood's spirit rocketed to the clouds. He took his red polka dot bandana off, stuffed it into the top of his front pocket and immediately put on the one she had given him.

"I have no gift for you."

"All I want is for you to come back alive." She leaned forward and lightly kissed him on the cheek. Her lips felt soft as rose petals against his skin. When she pulled away from him, Hood felt his old bandana slide from his pocket. He could feel his heart pounding in his chest and in his throat as he watched her tuck it away into the hip pocket of her dress. Hood wasn't sure what was bigger trouble—chasing outlaws or the way Katy made him feel.

Fudd rode up to Hood as he mounted up. When they caught eyes they both had grins they could hardly suppress. Hood said to Fudd, "You look like the cat that just swallowed the canary."

Fudd retorted delightfully, "Oh, it tasted much sweeter than that."

Hood's response?

"Royal."

They pulled the horses about and trotted to the waiting posse. As the posse pulled out of town, Hood and Fudd lapsed into silence. Their hearts were light, but the road ahead of them would be dangerous. They might come back heroes. Then again, they might not come back at all.

Veronica gathered her twins and Mother Fudd joined them as they watched the posse disappear into the forest. "We should pray for our men," Veronica suggested. They grabbed hands forming a small circle and did just that.

≫—34—→
THE SHOWDOWN

THE POSSE travelled south as the Sheriff led them out of Iron Gate. Within minutes, the Sheriff asked Hood to ride beside him. "I need you to tell me, again, everything you heard and saw when you encountered the outlaws making their plans."

Hood told the Sheriff how Emmett was the leader of the five outlaws, but the mysterious sixth horseman appeared to be the Boss. He also reiterated that he heard them speak of meeting up at Eagle Rock, and they spoke of train number eight.

"Well, the Colonel usually isn't a reliable source of information, but he was rather insistent that it was five outlaws that robbed the train." The Sheriff was speaking to the entire posse as they continued south toward Eagle Rock. "It would be good if we could verify that we are on the right trail. I suspect that they would take the mountain trail as opposed to the river trail due to the likelihood of running into other people."

"Might I suggest," said T.R., addressing the group, "that they have no reason to believe we know which direction they are going."

"Good point," chimed in Xavier.

"Well then, let's kick up some dust and kill us some outlaws," said Fletch, impatiently.

"Easy now, Fletch," implored the Sheriff. "It would be best if we were certain that we are on the villains' path."

When they reached the Rich Patch Mountain trail that led to Eagle Rock, the Sheriff ordered the posse to dismount and look for clues. Within seconds, Hood spoke up.

"Over here, Sheriff," Hood announced. The whole posse came over to look. "Right here, Sheriff, plain as day. Looks like six sets of hoof prints and one of the horses has a broken shoe."

Rigger spoke up, "I thought it was supposed to be five outlaws we were chasing."

"Maybe they have Madeline on the sixth horse," suggested Fudd. Then he called Buddy over and put Buddy's nose to the hoof prints. Buddy seemed to understand what Fudd was telling him. He let out a single bark.

"Let's make some tracks of our own, Sheriff." Fletch was already getting back in the saddle.

"Mount up, boys." The Sheriff mounted and turned to Hood. "Can you keep us on those tracks, Jedediah?"

"Yes, sir, Sheriff. That broken shoe will make it easy. We can ride a little faster than usual."

"Well then, take the lead."

Hood gave Thunder a "giddy-up" and the posse was off. Buddy shot ahead.

Hood and Thunder had formed an immediate bond and looked as if they had ridden together all their lives. As noon rolled around and the sun reached its zenith, the posse had worked up a pretty good sweat. Hood noticed a small clearing next to where a creek crossed the trail and raised his hand, letting out a soft "whoa." The posse came to a halt.

Hood dismounted and walked over to the remains of a small camp fire. He placed his hand on one of the stones that had ringed the fire. He could tell by the matted ash pile that water or coffee had been used to douse the flames. "Looks like they camped here last night, Sheriff," Hood informed him. "Also, the rocks are still warm; they got a late start."

Everyone dismounted except for Fletch who was still itchin' in the saddle. "Let's get a move on, Sheriff. I can feel it; we're close."

"We need to water the horses, Fletch. They have to be strong in case we get caught up in a chase."

Fletch knew that the Sheriff was right but he didn't care.

"But we're so close, Sheriff," Fletch protested. "Let's take down those heartless vermin." Fletch wore an expression of cold, hard steel. He also wore four pistols and carried two rifles.

Rigger walked over to Fletch and rubbed the muzzle of his horse. "We'll get her back, Fletch." He tried to reassure his friend. "We'll bring your little girl home."

Rigger had known Fletch since childhood. They had fought side by side at Appomattox, the last battle of the Civil War. He had been best man when Fletch married Millie. He had held Madeline in his arms as an infant. He was willing to die if it meant getting Madeline home alive.

The rest of the posse looked on in silence. T.R. noted the tone of compassion coming from this giant of a man. He'd ridden with some rough riders in his time, but he was very proud to ride with these men, to be a part of this posse.

Fletch mumbled something under his breath but dismounted his horse and walked him over to the creek. Rigger and Xavier followed.

Hood, Fudd, T.R. and Sheriff Green sat down by the dead campfire and gnawed at some jerky. T.R. took off his hat and used it to beat some trail dust off of his riding chaps. Buddy lay at Fudd's feet.

For a moment, nobody said anything. Then Fudd broke the silence. "I've never fired a gun at a man before."

"Shooting at a man is nothing you ever want to do," said the Sheriff. "Even killin' the most evil men will make a good man search his soul. But mark my words, young Mr. Fudd, these men will kill you or me or anyone else and not lose a wink of sleep. Unless they surrender, then you show them no mercy."

Both boys nodded in agreement.

Fudd and Hood both tossed Buddy a piece of jerky at the same time. Buddy caught Hood's piece. The friends made eye contact and smiled.

"Buddy's gonna wonder who his master is if you keep feedin' him," chided Fudd.

"Oh, I don't think that will ever be a problem. He still lies down at your feet," Hood retorted.

Buddy let loose a playful bark. He seemed to know that the conversation was about him.

Xavier, Fletch and Rigger led their horses up from the creek and joined the others by the old campfire. Xavier, always the provider, reached into his pack and brought out a loaf of bread he'd brought from home. He began breaking it into chunks and passing it around. The townsfolk had often wondered how Xavier managed to make money when he was always giving bargains to the people who needed them the most. Generosity was not a normal personality trait for a trading post owner.

The small talk continued as they ate. New bonds of friendship were being formed. Rigger started talking of the logging camp near Long Dale Furnace where he had been working the last few months.

Fudd jumped into the conversation. "My big brother is working in that camp. Have you met him?"

"What's his name?"

"Paul Fudd."

"The only Paul I know in that camp is Paul Bunyan."

"That would be him. Paul Bunyan Fudd."

"Paul Bunyan Fudd is your brother, eh?" said Rigger. "I reckon I can see the resemblance now that you mention it. In the short time your brother has been there, he has already earned himself a reputation as a top-notch logger."

"I'm not too surprised," said Fudd. "He has always been a hard worker."

"Everyone who works logging camps is a hard worker. That ain't nothin' special. Your brother saved the life of the foreman a few months back. A wagon with logs flipped and pinned the foreman underneath. One man dashed to get an ox to lift the weight. Bunyan said that it would take too long, so he lifted the wagon enough that the foreman could be pulled from underneath. He always wears a blue logging shirt so now everyone calls him 'The Blue Ox.'" Rigger smiled confidently. "He also came in second place in the logging games last month. It took all I had to keep that young upstart at bay."

Fudd beamed proudly, "Royal!"

Once everyone was sufficiently fed, the Sheriff stood and said, "Let's water the rest of the horses and be on our way."

Fletch was the first to his feet. He had remained quiet while everyone else bantered and swapped stories. The others stood, too, reminded once more of their reason for being there. The lighthearted mood had evaporated, leaving behind the harsh reality of their mission. There was a good chance that this day or the next, both good men and bad men would die. It was time to get serious.

★ ★ ★

Shotgun Staubach rode up next to Emmett. He'd been riding behind the others, keeping a lookout for a posse. He was very good at his job.

"We got a posse on our tail."

"How many and how far back?" Emmett's voice was cool and level. He was not surprised. He had secretly hoped the posse would catch up so he could use the opportunity to make off with the money. That was why they hadn't made great time or covered up their tracks.

"There are seven riders," Shotgun answered just as calmly. "They're less than a mile back."

"Have they spotted us?" asked Emmett.

"Don't think so," Shotgun responded.

Emmett just nodded his head.

Bubba and Irving had been listening, their faces tense with fear.

"Give us our cut now," implored Bubba. "We can ride two different directions and they won't be able to follow all of us." His voice quivered a little as he spoke.

Emmett rested his hand on the butt of his pistol. "Bubba and Irving, you boys are gonna have to fight if you want to get your share, so change your diapers. You can fight me right now and then fight the posse, or you can just fight the posse. If you ain't got the stomach for fightin' the law, then you can put your tail between your legs now and leave. But you ain't getting your cut."

Bubba and Irving knew that Emmett was quick on the draw. Neither wanted a showdown. Shotgun had moved his horse off to the side and seemed only mildly interested in the discussion. Lazarus didn't say a word, but he looked ready to draw. Madeline's eyes were wide with panic. She was perched on the money horse, which was tethered to Emmett's horse. If bullets started flying, she would be square in the middle of it.

The stalemate was broken when Irving finally said, "I guess we better fight the law. For this kind of money, I'll fight the law and the law won't win."

Lazarus lowered his hand from his holster and Madeline slumped forward a little in relief. Emmett had control of the gang once again. He also knew now how he was going to get away with the money.

Emmett surveyed his Cowboys. "We need to spring a trap."

★ ★ ★

The heat of the day was over and an evening chill was setting in. The posse had about an hour of light left. After that, it would be too dark to track.

"Let's push on 'til dark. We can make camp in the dark, and then continue at first light."

"Those Cowboys might keep ridin' after dark, Sheriff. We don't want to lose ground overnight," said Fletch.

"I'm sorry, Fletch," began the Sheriff. "We might end up gettin' further from their trail in the dark. Or we could lose it all together. And we got to rest the horses."

"They have to rest their horses, too," Xavier added.

"We'll get those vermin in the morning," said Rigger. "They can't be far."

Buddy froze on the trail up ahead of the posse, his nose turned up into the wind. Fudd and Hood both recognized his warning. Hood raised his right hand and brought the posse to a halt. Then he signaled for them to come in tight.

Fudd whispered to the Sheriff, "Buddy says that something is lurkin' in that pass."

"Do you think it's the outlaws?" asked Rigger.

"I can't say for sure," Fudd responded. "Buddy, here boy." He looked at the others. "If they are watching then I don't want them to know that Buddy made them." Buddy obeyed his master and retreated to the group.

"We have to assume that it is Emmett and the Cowboys," said T.R. "Look how the trail winds through the middle of the pass, with hills on either side. It is a prime spot for an ambush. There are some boulders and trees we could use for cover, but the outlaws would have good vantage points to fire down upon us. If they position themselves on both sides, then we would be pinned down in a cross fire."

"Agreed," said the Sheriff. "We need an advantage."

"We could make them think that they're getting what they want, Sheriff," Hood spoke up. "We could send three people slowly up the middle as a diversion. Then have pairs of men circle around both mountain tops. While the Cowboys are focused on the team coming up the middle, our other teams can surprise them from behind."

"I like the plan," said Fletch. "Whoever goes up the middle will be taking a big risk. I volunteer to be part of the diversion team."

Rigger spoke up next. "I'm going up the middle with Fletch." He looked over at his friend. "Just like old times. Right, Fletch?"

Fletch nodded in approval of his friend.

"I'll go too," volunteered Xavier.

"No," said the Sheriff. "They will be looking for me. They need to see me coming up the middle. Xavier, I want you to team up with Ruben, and circle the east peak. T.R., you and Jedediah take the west."

Hood spoke up again. "If someone were to see their horses left unguarded then the horses should be captured or run off. If they have no horses, then they can't escape."

"Good call, Jedediah," the Sheriff acknowledged. He looked over his posse with a stern gaze. "Does anyone have any questions?"

Everyone knew their part. Xavier took a slug of water from his canteen and handed it to Rigger. "Good luck, my friend," Xavier said.

Rigger raised the canteen in the manner of a toast.

★ ★ ★

Up ahead, the Cowboys watched from a gladed thicket as the posse came to a break.

"Did that dog make us?" Lazarus asked Emmett.

Emmett watched a little longer. The posse was still a good quarter mile down the trail with a fairly steep climb in front of them.

"I don't think so," he replied at last. "They seem to be taking a water break, and I can see the dog again. He's just hanging out with the rest of them."

More time went by with the Cowboys staring down at the resting posse, "This is a good spot for an ambush," Emmett announced to the gang. "They have to come up this pass. Bubba, you and Irving take the mound on the western ridge. Lazarus, you and Shotgun take the rock cropping on the eastern slope. One of you position high and the other a bit lower. When they get within range, cut 'em to ribbons. I'll take the horses and the girl around to the south side of the peak, so they don't get hit by any stray bullets. Then I'll climb over the edge to where I can fire down on the posse as well."

The Cowboys spread out and took up their positions. Everything was working out as Emmett had schemed. Once he was out of their view, he moved the saddle bags of money from Madeline's horse to his own. Madeline just stared at him stoically as he went about his task, her hands tied and her mouth gagged. She could still be used as a shield if it was necessary.

Emmett now had all the Cowboy's horses. When the shooting started, he could just ride off with the money and the horses. If the posse won the fight, then they would be dealing with the dead and the wounded. If the Cowboys won the battle, then they would use the horses from the posse and come after him. In either case, he would keep going after dark, hide his trail and change directions. Yes, the fight would keep everyone very busy. He might not even have to kill the girl. He felt benevolent now that he was a man of wealth. From his vantage point he watched as a horse and rider came into view near the bottom of the pass. Moments later a second horse and rider, and then a third emerged.

★ ★ ★

Sheriff Green saw a slight movement in the trees up ahead. Without turning his head, he whispered, "I see one up ahead, on the right." He brought his horse to a halt and casually dismounted. Fletch and Rigger did the same. Then, without warning, they dashed for cover in the rocks and trees along the bottom of the pass.

★ ★ ★

Irving was so nervous he was about to jump out of his skin. Unconsciously, he had shuffled from foot to foot as the posse had approached. He stood behind a pine tree with the barrel of his rifle pressed to its side to steady his aim. He was midway down the slope. His only comfort was that Bubba protected his flank from a position higher above. The posse was just getting into range. He wanted a closer shot. He followed the second rider with the bead of his sight. They stopped and dismounted so casually that he'd assumed they were going to stretch their legs. It didn't occur to him that the posse had just taken such a break. When the men suddenly dashed for cover, Irving panicked, but recovered quickly. He took aim at one of the fleeing figures and squeezed off a shot.

Fletch saw the bullet kick up dirt just to his right. The report from the gun was deafening; he knew the shooter had to be close. He dove for cover between two large boulders that bordered the trail on the western slope. He could feel his heart beat in his throat as bullets ricocheted and sparks flew just above his head.

Lazarus had a perfect burrow in the rocks from which to fight. He was protected from all sides. He had that big logger guy directly in his sights. Just before he was ready to shoot, he was distracted by Irving's premature shot. "Irving!" he thought as he looked across the ravine. "That coward panicked and shot too early." Lazarus quickly refocused on the logger as he ran for cover and squeezed off a shot.

Rigger dashed for a large oak that stood near the bottom of the eastern slope. As he dove for the base of the tree, he felt a bullet rip through his thigh, just above his knee. He scrambled to a sitting position and flattened his back against the trunk. Blood was oozing from the wound freely, and he could feel the sticky warmth as it flowed down his leg. He pulled the bandana from his neck and cinched it tightly over the wound. Rigger took large gulps of air, trying to calm his beating heart as more bullets pounded both sides of the mighty oak, bark fragments raining on his head. He tucked his knees to his chest to keep his legs out of the line of fire. He couldn't move in either direction without taking another bullet. He was pinned down completely. Flashbacks of the Civil War flooded his memory.

Sheriff Green dashed ahead for a deadfall that bordered the trail. A large root ball attached to the trunk of the tree provided a small sanctuary. He watched in horror as his horse dropped dead in the middle of the trail, and the other horses fled the way they had come.

He could feel the impact of bullet after bullet pounding into the dirt ball that protected him. Between volleys, he popped up and squeezed off a few round of his own to force the outlaws to duck for cover. Fletch followed his lead, and the onslaught of the initial attack was slowed.

★ ★ ★

Emmett smiled wickedly when the first shot rang out. He turned to Madeline and flashed his fourteen-karat grin. "We are out of here, my darlin'; a better life awaits us." All of the horses were tethered together in a line, each horse's reins tied to the saddle of the horse in front of it. He spurred his horse on and led Madeline and the caravan away from the battle.

Madeline wanted no part of any life that involved Emmett Stone. She was more mad than scared. She struggled with her bindings, but they were tightly secured to the saddle horn.

★ ★ ★

Shotgun watched from his perch above Lazarus. He hadn't fired a shot. He thought he had the posse's plan figured out when only three riders came up the middle of the pass. He was tucked behind a deadfall and had a view of the battle below, the opposite ridge, his flank and Emmett's position. He was also close to a small ravine that could be used as an escape route if the situation arose. He didn't like that Emmett was in control of his horse one bit, but with the posse bearing down on them, he had to go along with the plan. As he watched his flank, he saw a kid and a well-dressed rider dashing over the mountain top. They were both wearing deputy stars. "Too bad for them." He leveled his Sharps' Big Bore on the kid because he was closest to discovering his position. He would only shoot if the kid made him. Then he caught sight of Emmett making his move. "Lucky kid," he thought, backing into his escape ravine and taking off after Emmett.

Hood's heart was racing as they came over the top of the western ridge. He could hear one of the Cowboys pumping off shots just below him, but a boulder was protecting the shooter from view. He flashed a sign to T.R. and pointed to the location of the shooter, but T.R. had the same problem. The Cowboy was too well concealed. Then Hood caught a movement in the distance. Horses were moving in the tree line and he caught a glimpse of Emmett and Madeline. Hood dashed recklessly to where T.R. was positioned. Panting excitedly, he said "I just saw Emmett making his escape! He's ditching out on his partners. I'm runnin' back to get Thunder."

"Don't worry about Emmett right now," protested T.R. "We have to help out the Sheriff. They're pinned in a cross-fire down below."

"Emmett has Madeline."

T.R.'s eyes widened with the dilemma, and he quickly recalculated, "You go after Madeline, and I'll help the Sheriff. I'll come after you as soon as we have the situation under control."

"Good luck," Hood called back as he was already running down the mountain.

★ ★ ★

Bubba watched from his perch above Irving. The element of surprise was gone, but they had three members of the posse pinned down. He fired volley after volley at all three positions to keep it that way. The rest of the posse must be trying to out-flank them, he figured. He scanned the woods, looking for movement. He decided he'd best sit quiet for a spell and wait for them to come to him. Then he saw Xavier, the Trading Post owner. "Looks like there's gonna be a job opening in town," he cackled to himself.

Xavier ran along quickly in a crouch. The shooting had started and he knew that the diversion team needed help from above. He had his Winchester repeater gripped tightly in his hand and a pistol in the holster on his hip for backup. He slowed as he neared the crest. The battle was raging below him. He could see Irving firing wildly into the ravine, so he calmly leveled his gun on him. Xavier felt like a sniper, shooting at someone who wasn't aiming at him, but this man was making shot after shot, trying to kill his friends. In the frenzy and focus of the moment, Xavier never even heard the shot. All he felt was a burning sensation in his hip. The force of the blow sent him sprawling and his rifle flew from his hand. He tried to get up and run, but his right leg wouldn't do what his mind commanded. One of the Cowboys was walking toward him with a wicked grin and a pointed rifle. Xavier pulled his pistol and it fell apart in his hand. The bullet in his hip had gone through the pistol first.

"Say your prayers, Trader Man," Bubba snarled as he cocked his rifle.

Now it was Bubba's turn to be taken by surprise. Just as his rifle erupted, a sudden blow knocked the gun from his grip. Buddy's teeth tore into Bubba's forearm just below the elbow. He watched as the dog hit the ground tumbling, pivoted as it regained its feet and mounted another charge. Bubba adeptly drew his pistol and BOOM!

Buddy disengaged the attack.

Bubba watched in disbelief as the small stain in the middle of his own chest began to spread. He looked to his left and there stood Fudd with a smoking pistol. "Funny," he thought, "it don't even hurt." Then he thought, "A kid…I been killed by a kid." He whipped around and fired.

Fudd fired, too.

Bubba was blown off his feet, and Fudd hit the ground grimacing in pain. Flat on his back, he stared up at the sky for a moment before Buddy came over to lick his face, whimpering. He sat up and reassured his dog by grabbing his face in both hands and pulling it toward his own. "It's all right boy, it's all right. You did great, boy." Blood was running from his bicep. After a quick examination, Fudd got to his feet and checked on Xavier.

The hail of fire pinning the posse to the bottom of the pass began to let up. The Sheriff and Fletch were returning fire with more accuracy, as they could occasionally peek out from behind their cover. Rigger had even gotten off a few volleys of his own.

Lazarus and Irving both sensed they had lost their partners positioned above them, but they had no choice but to battle on.

Both sides of the combat were startled when Hood and Thunder charged through the middle of the pass like a bolt of lightning.

★ ★ ★

Emmett was giddy with excitement. All was going according to plan. If by chance a pursuit was mounted, he could cut the tether line to the girl's horse and it would be just him and the money. He felt a drag from behind as the tether line tightened. The little spitfire was slowing down her horse. Emmett dug the spurs deep into his horse's belly and they were moving along again.

Madeline was determined to escape. She tugged with all of her might at the knot that bound her hands to the saddle horn and it slipped over the top. She reached for the bandana that gagged her mouth and yanked it out of the way. "Daddy!" she shrieked at the top of her lungs. "Help me, DADDY!"

Emmett felt a searing rage rush into his brain. How dare that girl try to defy him in his moment of glory? Well, he had warned her time and again. He whipped around pistol in hand, and Madeline froze in terror. "You truly are more trouble than you are worth," he said as he spun the cylinder of his pistol and leveled it at her face.

★ ★ ★

When Fletch Gordon heard his daughter's scream, he became oblivious to the bullets hissing all around him. He burst from his cover, running with pistols clutched tightly in both hands.

"Fletch, get down," Sheriff Green yelled, but Fletch was not to be detained.

On the opposite ridge, Irving stepped away from his pine tree and drew a bead on Fletch as he ran. Fletch caught the movement in the corner of his eye, spun and cut loose two shots with each pistol in rapid succession. Irving dropped to his knees before he could get off a shot. Fletch didn't even slow down. The sound of his daughter's voice drew him like a magnet.

Lazarus's ideal firing position had one major downfall. It was in a direct path between Fletch and his daughter. Madeline kept screaming. Fletch kept advancing. Lazarus kept shooting. T.R., Fudd, Xavier, Sheriff Green and Rigger watched in amazement as Fletch ducked and dived from one boulder or tree to the next. Lazarus finally panicked and popped out of his burrow like a rabbit. He hadn't retreated two paces when Fletch shot him in the left buttock. Lazarus fell to the ground and his pistol hit the dust in front of him. As Fletch ran past him, he kicked the gun out of reach, leaving the wailing Cowboy for the others to deal with.

Madeline knew she was about to die. She thought of her sister—they could do their chores together again, in heaven.

"You shoot that little girl, Emmett, and I'll shoot you dead." Emmett whirled around to see Shotgun Staubach standing in the path ahead of him, his pistol aimed at Emmett's chest. "Why don't you cut the tether line on those horses nice and slow."

Emmett drew his knife slowly with his left hand. "Grab a horse, Shotgun, we can be out of here with the money. Let's go."

"I think I'll take all the horses, Emmett. Yours too, with the money."

At that moment, Madeline rolled off her horse and dashed away from Emmett. The distraction gave Emmett a chance to draw on Shotgun—and he did.

Shotgun realized instantly that he had lost his advantage and dove to his right. He was hit in his left shoulder. Madeline scrambled behind a boulder and Emmett had no clear shot so he let her go. He slashed the tether line, freeing his horse from the others, and took off at a full gallop.

Shotgun staggered to his feet and yelled over to Madeline, "You okay, little girl?"

"Yeah," Madeline gasped, still breathless. She remained hidden behind the rock.

"Getting you into this mess wasn't my idea."

"I know, mister. Thanks for saving my life."

She peeked over the edge of the boulder and watched as he grabbed his horse's reins with his good arm, blood staining the shoulder of his other arm. He swung himself up into the saddle and spurred the animal forward, but not in the direction Emmett had gone.

Madeline watched him disappear into the evening mist. She could tell he was injured pretty badly. "That might be the end of that man," she thought to herself.

Suddenly, she heard the pounding of hoof beats and turned to see Hood riding up hard to the scene like a knight on a joust. "You all right, Madeline?" Hood asked as he and Thunder skidded to a halt. Thunder reared slightly. He was enjoying the pursuit.

Madeline nodded her head. Her heart, already faint with excitement, fluttered a little at the sight of Hood charging to the rescue.

Hood had seen the shoot-out between Emmett and Shotgun and had seen the two men head off in different directions. He was going after Emmett. "Your daddy is here. Tell the others I'm on Emmett's trail."

Madeline nodded once.

Thunder reared up again, and then he and Hood galloped down the trail after Emmett.

Hood was scarcely out of sight when a familiar voice called out the little girl's name. Madeline turned her head to the sound. "Here I am, Daddy. Oh, here I am!"

THE CHASE

EMMETT WAS riding as hard as his horse could run. The extra weight of the gold and silver coins was slowing him down. He hadn't put nearly the distance between him and the scene of the gunfight that he would have liked. His horse would not last long at this pace. He needed to get up into the very steep peaks of Rich Patch Mountain and get lost from the posse in the dark of night. He could walk his horse through the steeps and the horse wouldn't get worn out. The posse would have to do the same and they would have trouble making up ground on him before night set in. Emmett turned his horse off of the trail and toward the upper peaks. He took one final look back to see if the posse was in view. He strained his eyes in the waning light. At first he saw nothing, just the colored mist. Then, just as he was turning away, a figure cut through the mist. A single rider wearing a bowler hat was coming up hard. It was Hood. His heart skipped a beat, and then he smiled.

Hood watched as Emmett turned up into the mountains. He had made up a lot of ground. It was a smart move on Emmett's part to take the chase up into the cliffs. Hood had to stop him before dark; the terrain would soon become too treacherous to ride. Before long, Hood found Emmett's boot prints where he had jumped off of his horse to lead it. He jumped off as well.

The deer path they were following wound around ravines and spines and all sorts of crevasses. The view from up here was magnificent, and he was only halfway up. All the smaller peaks and valleys near the river were dwarfed at this height. Hood could see the peaks of the Blue Ridge Mountain range in the distance, across the Shenandoah Valley. They seemed to float in a blue haze as twilight set in. "Easy to tell how they got their name," he thought.

An ambush would be easy in this terrain. Hood was forced to take his time. He didn't like the position he was in. If he went too slowly, he would lose Emmett in the dark and Emmett could just slip away and never be seen again. If he went too fast, then he could walk right into a bullet. He had no choice but to push forward cautiously.

The trail flattened out about halfway up the ridge. Hood mounted Thunder and rode out into a small meadow. At the other end of the meadow was Emmett Stone. Their eyes locked and Emmett kicked his horse into a mad gallop. He disappeared down a trail into the woods and around a bend.

Hood leaned forward and Thunder bolted after Emmett in hot pursuit. They rounded the bend at full speed. Thunder seemed to glide as the branches whisked past. Hood's bowler hat blew off his head, but for the moment he did not care. He gripped his Winchester in his right hand and Thunder's reins and mane in his left. He was leaning so far forward that his neck was touching Thunder's. He felt weightless with exhilaration, almost as if he was flying.

Then he saw the rope stretched across the trail. It was a trap and it had been expertly sprung. Hood yanked back on the reins and Thunder slammed on the brakes. The rope hit Thunder square across the chest and the jolt sent Hood flying forward off of Thunder's back. Hood landed on his hands and knees, skidded, rolled once and came to a stop with his face to the ground.

Emmett stepped out from behind a tree with his pistol drawn. "I was hopin' to see you one more time before I left these parts, Half-Breed." He spat out the last words and then flashed his gold front teeth in a foul sneer.

Hood lifted himself to his hands and knees.

Emmett took a few steps forward and planted himself directly in front of Hood. "You know," he said, scratching his chin with his free hand in mock thoughtfulness, "I got paid to kill your father. Did you know that?"

Hood glared up at him in silence.

"Yessir," Emmett continued, "I got good money for that job. But as for you, I'm gonna kill you just for fun."

Hood's palms burned where they had skidded through the sandy soil.

Emmett smiled again and said, "Looks like it's time to send you to that spirit in the sky."

Hood stared up into Emmett's gleaming eyes and stated, "I know that's where I'm going when I die."

Emmett spun the cylinder on his pistol.

"Because I have a friend in Jesus!" Hood exclaimed, and clenched two fists full of dirt and whipped them into Emmett's face.

Emmett staggered backwards and his gun went off just as Hood dove and rolled hard to his right. Hood felt no pain, and came out of his roll with the blade of his knife in his hand, ready for battle. Emmett was wiping his eyes with his left sleeve and bringing his pistol around on Hood with his right. While Emmett was in motion, Hood aimed low and hurled the knife, planting it solidly into his right thigh. He jumped and rolled one more time, wondering briefly why he hadn't buried the knife into Emmett's heart.

Emmett screamed in pain and started firing his gun wildly in Hood's direction. Hood ducked into the cover of the woods, knowing he, at last, had the advantage.

Emmett staggered after him, screaming obscenities and insults at the top of his lungs. He fired more shots into the darkening woods, even though he didn't have a target. He bled and seethed and flailed about like a man possessed, the knife still protruding from his thigh. Then, suddenly, he remembered his horse and whipped around to locate it. Both the horse with the money and Thunder were gone.

Hood made his way downhill, away from Emmett's screams. He assessed his situation. He had both horses and the money and Emmett was wounded, so things were looking pretty good—but as long as Emmett had a gun and any fight left in him, he was still dangerous. Hood's own gun and knife were gone now, but his bow and arrows were still strapped to Thunder's saddle. He unlashed his only weapon. He hoped he'd cross paths with the posse soon. As he continued down the mountain, Emmett's words echoed in Hood's head: *I got paid to kill your father.*

★ ★ ★

Sheriff Green tended to Xavier's and Rigger's wounds. Xavier was doing better than initially thought because the bullet hit his pistol before it entered his hip. He was hobbled, but he could move around on his own. Rigger, on the other hand, had lost a good bit of blood. He was turning pale and his friends were getting concerned.

Fudd had gone up into the rocks and dragged Lazarus down to the trail and tied his hands behind his back. Lazarus hadn't stopped running his mouth the whole time and Fudd was ready to gag him.

T.R climbed the western ridge to check on Bubba and Irving. He came back with his report. "Both of those boys are dead."

Fudd's heart sank as he looked at his hands. He had killed a man.

Xavier put his hand on Fudd's shoulder. "I have never seen a clearer case of self-defense."

Fudd nodded but continued to look at his shooting hand. He felt like it was stained with blood.

"You saved my life, Buddy's life and your own."

"I know," Fudd looked up at Xavier. "I just keep seein' his face in my mind. He looked so bewildered, like he couldn't believe it."

Fletch walked back with Madeline perched in his right arm. Her feet had yet to touch the ground. He had captured the string of horses and led them back with his free hand. He walked over to where Rigger lay and asked, "How are you, my friend?"

Rigger looked up to see Madeline in Fletch's arms, and his pale face brightened.

"Better now." The words took effort to expel.

Madeline began to squirm and he set her down. She sat next to Rigger and grabbed for his hand. His eyes glowed as he looked into hers; her hand was swallowed by his mighty paw. Tears rolled down her face as she feared for this man she had known since birth.

"We got to get Rigger to the doctor," announced the Sheriff, stating the obvious.

"I need a doctor, *toooo*," whined Lazarus.

"Shut up!" Xavier, Fudd and the Sheriff all said at once.

"But my arse! I have a bullet in my arse!"

Buddy walked over and put his muzzle next to Lazarus's face, baring his teeth in a growl.

Lazarus shut up.

"I have to go help Jedediah." T.R. stated as he looked at the Sheriff and waited for approval.

The Sheriff nodded.

"Me too," Fudd quickly volunteered.

"Sorry, son, I'm gonna need you. We got a lot of wounded here, including you. We also have a prisoner." The Sheriff could tell that Fudd was upset. "Rigger's life hangs in the balance."

Fudd nodded in acceptance of the situation. "I understand, Sheriff."

T.R. quickly retrieved his horse, Pepper. As he rode back by the group, he stopped and wished them all well. "Fight the good fight, Rigger," he said and he tipped his hat in a salute.

The corners of Rigger's lips lifted in a smile, "I just did."

T.R. galloped after Hood.

Night was creeping in, and T.R. wasn't sure how he would find Hood and Emmett. Then he heard a gunshot. The battle had been taken into the upper peaks. "I guess that's how," he said aloud. Three more shots rang out, and he drove Pepper harder, hoping he wasn't already too late.

★ ★ ★

Dusk was prime hunting time for the big she lion, but tonight her lust to kill was especially strong. The scent of blood hung heavy in the air. She sensed the danger and death all about her, and she wanted her turn. Gunshots didn't scare her any more. She knew what they did. She had eaten the remains left over by hunters plenty of times. She slinked onwards, following the scent of gunpowder and man. A great horned owl swooped by to her left. It made no sound. The squirrel had no chance. She considered taking the squirrel from the owl but quickly ruled it out. She wanted her own kill, so she continued on. The clamor of gunfire had ceased, but she knew she was close. Then, she saw her victim.

Emmett had quit screaming and was now scheming on a plan to draw Hood back to him. He needed a horse if he was going to get out of this alive—preferably, the money horse. He might also have a chance to grab a horse from another posse member. At this point, any horse would do. He heard a sudden noise and looked up.

Hood figured the posse to be a short distance away. They had to have heard all those shots. He just needed to stay clear of Emmett until reinforcements arrived. That was when he heard the mountain lion scream. Emmett heard it too. And then a shot.

The mountain lion screamed as she leapt from her rock ledge onto T.R.'s back. She was going for the neck.

T.R. heard the cry and twisted violently in his saddle, giving the cat a mouthful of shoulder. He cried out in pain as he toppled from his horse and slammed into the ground chest first. The force of the impact broke the lion's grip, and T.R. rolled away. The cat let out another ear-splitting yowl.

Pepper was spooked and throwing kicks in every direction. T.R.

174

looked up just in time to see two sharp hooves bearing down on him. He dove left, and came up with his pistol drawn and aimed at the cat. Just as he fired, though, Pepper's rear hooves flew skyward, connecting with his outstretched hand.

The lion let out a furious scream. Her back hip burned and blood seeped down her leg. She stared fiercely at her prey as he knelt, clutching his empty hand. The horse bucked wildly in between them. She stalked left, then right. She could smell the fear of the crazed animal and his defenseless rider. Then the horse bolted, leaving her victim exposed. She charged.

Hood rode up on the scene as fast as Thunder could carry him. He jerked Thunder's reins and launched himself from the saddle with his bow and three arrows in his grasp. He hit the ground running and knocked up the first arrow just as Pepper bolted and the cat lunged. He slid to a stop on both knees and released an arrow.

T.R. watched as the beast barreled down on him. There was nowhere to run. He clenched his fists together and swung them like a club at the cat's massive head. As she sprung, her paws stretched out before her. He heard a sickening *thunk* as the beast struck his shoulders, knocking him to his back. He could feel her hot breath wash over his face and the sting of her teeth bearing down on his neck. Just when T.R. thought he was on an express train to his Maker, her grip slackened and she rolled limply away from him.

T.R. scrambled to his feet and stared in amazement at the arrow protruding from the mountain lion's chest. He let out a choked laugh when he turned his head to see Hood casually strolling over to where he stood. "It looks like you hit her in the lungs." He shook his head in disbelief as he'd expected to be dead by now. "Good shot."

The beast was alive but gasping for breath. They took a few steps back as she struggled to regain her feet. Then her legs buckled and the lion collapsed, the life gone from her, her reign of terror expired.

"How bad are you hurt?" Hood asked, turning his attention back to his friend.

"Broke wrist and a few scratches. I feel pretty good about the way it all turned out, actually. I owe that to you."

Hood beamed momentarily, but was quick to remember that there was still one problem left to deal with. "We need to gather all the horses," Hood began. "Emmet is nearby. He has a cut up leg and no horse–"

"I have a horse," a familiar voice cut Hood off, and Emmett limped out of the dusk, his pistol drawn. "In fact, I have two, if you include the money horse." He was leading Thunder with the money horse tethered behind. Emmett glanced down at the dead mountain lion and said sarcastically, "Nice shot, Half-Breed."

Emmett sneered at Hood in the dim light. Hood was glad he couldn't see those stupid gold teeth.

"I can hardly wait to kill you, boy," Emmett began as he dropped the reins and paced toward Hood and T.R. His left hand came up to spin the cylinder of his pistol.

"Hey, Emmett. I got the money horse now."

Emmett stopped in his tracks and whirled around.

Shotgun Staubach eased out from behind a tree, his pistol aimed right at his former leader. "Drop the gun, Emmett."

Emmett was slow to comply. He flashed what he thought was his most winning smile, but his eyes looked desperate. "Come on, Shotgun. Grab a horse. We can ride out of here and split the money. Split it right down the middle."

"I guess if we're doin' things even-steven, then I owe you a bullet."

Emmett dropped his gun.

T.R. and Hood relaxed for a second and Shotgun turned his attention back to them. "Not so fast. Don't make a play on any weapons. I'd rather not kill you."

Shotgun picked up Emmett's pistol and stuffed it into his belt. He eased back toward the horses. "I'm gonna take ten percent of the money. That's what the reward would be from the railroad." He slashed one of the saddlebags and grabbed two sacks of coins. Never once did he lower his gun.

With the money in hand, Shotgun whistled for his horse. The animal trotted over to him, and he put the coins in his saddlebag and mounted up. "You can have that worthless Cowboy," he gestured disdainfully at Emmett. "He's a backstabber, and he hides behind little girls." He gathered up his reins. "Tell the judge that I helped. Oh, and it would be best if y'all didn't try to come after me," he warned.

"I can only tell the judge what you did," T.R. responded. "I can't speak for the Sheriff either on this matter."

Shotgun smiled wryly and shrugged. "I guess that will have to do." He started to turn his horse away, then paused and looked back at Hood. "Nice shot, kid." With that, he gave his horse a swift spur and disappeared into the darkness.

Hood smiled. "Royal."

≫—36—→

HOME AGAIN

ROANOKE TIMES, *Wednesday, October 16, 1888*
"Posse Nabs Train Robbers and Mountain Lion!" read the headline. Papers across the country were running the story of the adventures taking place in Iron Gate and Glen Wilton.

"I can hardly believe that T.R. is really Theodore Roosevelt," Jeannie Cleary said as she lowered the newspaper she'd been reading to the class. "He's been in the news before. My daddy says that he will be president one day." She handed the paper to Lenny.

"He just told me to call him T.R.," Hood said. "I never knew his real name." Hood was a guest of honor in Miss Summers's classroom today.

Students were taking turns reading the paper and hearing direct tales of the adventure from Hood and Fudd. Buddy even made an appearance in several of the stories, including the one in the *Roanoke Times*. He sat at Fudd's feet and barked every time he heard his name. He wasn't usually allowed in the classroom, but today was a special day.

Lenny read an article that featured the individuals who were members of the posse. The paper had revealed T.R.'s true identity. He, Pepper and the mountain lion were on their way back to New York.

The Appalachian mountain lion would join his ever-growing collection of great beasts of the world.

Hood had received the bounty money on Emmett and the mountain lion. This would enable him to rebuild his family's cabin and hopefully rebuild his life.

Rigger survived his wound and was already spreading the story of the charge of "Flash" Gordon. Soon every logging camp and saloon throughout the Appalachians would be telling heroic stories attributed to that name.

Xavier Duran was recovering well from his bullet wound. He accepted as little credit as he could, modestly deflecting attention from himself. He was quoted in the paper: "I am just proud to have been a member of that posse and to have witnessed, first hand, the heroic 'Charge of "Flash" Gordon.'"

Fletch "Flash" Gordon's true reward was the safe return of his daughter. He also received everlasting fame that he didn't particularly care for. He was credited the reward for Irving and Lazarus, but insisted that Lazarus's reward would go to his friend, Jon Rigger.

Fudd and Buddy received the reward for Bubba. There was a small picture of Buddy inserted alongside the article that showed the Deputy badge pinned to his bandage.

The official listed recipient of the reward for the return of the coal-miners' money was Shotgun Staubach. The article was fuzzy as to how that came about. It wasn't mentioned in the paper, but the locals knew that Shotgun had a hand in saving Madeline. No effort was ever made to chase him down.

The whole community was beaming with pride. The bravery displayed by every member of the posse was quickly becoming legendary. The papers were eating it up. Some of the articles still described Hood as a "half-breed Cherokee," but now they treated the term like a compliment. They praised him for his superior tracking skills that led the posse to the outlaws and his ability to take down the man-eating mountain lion with a single arrow. They even noted, "His father, Jake

Hood, was Irish." Sequoia and Cher were also mentioned by name. The papers hadn't had this much fun since Jesse James got gunned down six years before, or maybe the shootout at the O.K. Corral, two years ago.

Lenny handed the paper to Katy. Her eyes glowed as she looked at Hood. Lenny felt all remaining hope of making Katy his own vanish. Hood was a hero, and she only had eyes for him. Katy turned to take the paper from Lenny and their eyes met. She seemed to know just what he was thinking. She gave him a soft, kind smile and Lenny blushed a little and felt better about everything. He liked Hood too. He was a good guy as well as a hero.

Katy looked at the picture of Hood on the front page. "You have to see your picture," she said, as she walked the paper to him.

A broad smile spread over Hood's face as he looked down at the photograph. There he was on the front page of the *Roanoke Times* with T.R. and the dead mountain lion. In the picture, he looked like a young man. He wished that his dad could have seen this picture. Then, his gaze drifted down to another picture on the lower, right-hand corner of the page and the smile froze on his face. He couldn't believe his eyes. Staring back up at him was the Boss who had met Emmett and the Cowboys in the woods just before the train robbery. The caption read: "John Brown runs unopposed for reelection as Sheriff of Roanoke: *The Town of Brown*."

★ ★ ★

Sheriff John Brown threw his newspaper down on his massive desk. He was furious. The paper slid across the desktop and fluttered in pieces to the floor.

Sheriff Brown's political advisor and assistant, Mr. Thadeus James, scurried around the room gathering it up.

"Nothing can be done about it now, Boss," Thadeus tried to ease him out of his tirade.

"BULL HOCKEY!" bellowed Sheriff Brown. "That boy has cost me money! He has removed some of my enforcers. And he has drawn sympathy for the 'Indian people.'" He said the last two words with disdain. "He has already caused more problems than his father ever did."

An instant later, Sheriff Brown had calmed himself. He continued on in a voice so collected that it scared Thadeus just a bit.

"I have positioned myself to be Sheriff of Roanoke for a second term. I expect to be running for Governor in four years. My platform has and will continue to be placing these savages in reservations. They are like vermin, threatening the comfort and safety of our communities, and right now most people agree with me. I'm even working on a deal to send our local tribes to a reservation down in North Carolina. If Hood creates sympathy for the tribes, then I will lose votes. That cannot be allowed to happen." The Sheriff smoothed his thinning hair back over his head and smiled. "We must come up with a very special solution for Mr. Jedediah Hood."

★ ★ ★

"Are you okay, Jedediah?" Miss Summers broke Hood out of his trance. He glanced up from the paper to find the whole class staring at him. Fudd was giving him a quizzical look.

"Couldn't be better," Hood assured them with a thoughtful, wily expression on his face. He began backing towards the door. "Fudd, we'll talk after school? I've got to go see Larry Stewart." He started to turn away, but stopped and looked back into the room.

As Hood stood before the room full of friendly, concerned faces, a warm feeling stole over him. They accepted him. He glanced down at his deerskin vest—which fit him now—at his Pops's old boots and the tattered bowler hat he held in his hands. These odd clothes had never felt more comfortable. He looked like a half-breed, and these were his friends.

He flashed a smile and said, "Things just keep gettin' better all the time." And he was gone.